Featherbys

Mary Steele

PEACHTREE

ATLANTA

JR
A Peachtree Junior Publication

Published by
PEACHTREE PUBLISHERS, LTD.
494 Armour Circle NE
Atlanta, Georgia 30324

First published in 1993 by Hyland House Publishing Pty Limited

Manufactured in the United States of America

10 9 8 7 6 5 4 3 2 1
First Edition

Library of Congress Cataloging-in-Publication Data
Steele, Mary.
Featherbys / by Mary Steele. — 1st ed.
        p. cm.
Summary: Jess thinks she is facing a boring vacation, when she and her friends
discover Featherbys.
        ISBN 1-56145-135-5 (pb)
        [1. Australia—Fiction.] I. Title.
        PZ7.S8145Fe   1996
        [Fic]—dc20

                                                96-14402
                                                CIP
                                                AC

Chapter 1

When our neighbor Mrs. Fontana died last year in a road accident, the old Miss Featherbys sent a card. My friend Sophie Fontana showed it to me after her mother's funeral. Miss Alice Featherby had written it.

Miss Featherby's handwriting was all stiff and old-fashioned, and so were the things she said on the card, like, "May I offer condolences on behalf of my sister and myself to Mr. Fontana, Sophia, and Roberto in their grievous loss"—or something like that.

It sounded rather starchy to me, but at least she knew what to say. I couldn't think of any of the right words to use to the Fontanas when everything was so awful for them. I just burst into tears and said I was sorry—and I was. Mrs. Fontana was a lovely person. Why did *she* have to be the one who was hit by the drunk driver?

Mr. Fontana kept the Featherbys' condolence card on the mantelpiece for ages. I suppose those words "grievous loss" seemed exactly right to him. When you think about them, they were exactly right coming from Miss Alice Featherby, but they would have sounded all wrong if *I'd* said them to Sophie. Different words seem to suit different people, like clothes.

Mr. Fontana is a builder, and one day when he was staring at the Featherbys' card he said, "I suppose I should offer to mend their fence pickets for them, poor old ducks, but I never seem to have time these days." He sighed. He was always sighing, because he and Sophie were having to run the house and to cook and look after Robbo and all those things, after Mrs. Fontana had died. I didn't blame him for being gloomy.

Robbo is Sophie's young brother and he's about the same age as my brother Ben. Mum often says, "You know, Jess, you and Ben are so fortunate to have kids of your own age next door. It's wonderful to have friends *so close!*" She is right, I guess, but the really amazing thing is that we *liked* each other from the start. Sophie and Robbo could have been real toads, or they might have thought that we were ratbrains and chucked garbage at us over the fence. We don't go to the same school either, but we are really good friends, especially during vacations.

The only problem is that Ben and I have a little sister, Vicky, and there is nobody of five next door for her to play with, so she is always trailing around after us and being a pain.

Before we really got to know the old Featherby ladies, the five of us kids were rather spooked by them. Sophie and I tried to work out why some old people put you off like that. We made a list of things we didn't like about old people, which we called our Geriatric List…

They wear black a lot—

They shuffle around on sticks—

They can be crabby and disapproving—

They always think things were better when they were young—

They ask dumb questions about school—

They haven't a clue about computers and VCRs and things—

They are deaf and you have to shout at them, which is embarrassing, and most of them don't understand what you are saying even if they aren't deaf—

They have wrinkled and saggy skin and yellow teeth (or no teeth at all, and then their lips are sucked in)—

Some old people even dribble. YUK!

We weren't really sure how many of these descriptions fitted the Featherbys because we hardly ever saw the old ladies, even though they lived close by. Their old place was at the back of ours, and it was always called *Featherbys* in the neighborhood.

They had a weekly grocery order delivered from the local shop, and sometimes Miss Violet slipped out early in the morning—we would see her as we went to school. She'd push open the rusty gate and scuttle like a gray mouse to Rudd's convenience store in the next street for a small carton of milk, but she was home again in no time as if she were scared of being seen. Miss Violet was the younger sister and she seemed to do the jobs and errands. Miss Alice never went out. She was well over eighty, Mum said. At least Miss Violet wore a gray coat, not black, and she didn't use a stick, but the way the two sisters lived was creepy, all alone in their ancient house under its huge, dark trees. It was almost as if they lived on another planet.

Sometimes Ben and Robbo would kick their soccer ball over the fence into *Featherbys*, or Sophie and I would feel like having a snoop, so we'd squeeze through one of the gaps in our back fences and find ourselves in a dim, dank wilderness. Every step we took crunched, so we'd drop onto all fours and crawl over the tangles of peri-winkle and ivy, and if we felt daring enough to go close to the old house and the backyard we'd wriggle flat on our stomachs like army guerrillas.

Usually there was nothing much to see or hear, but once when the boys were in there Miss Violet had ap-peared through the back doorway with a mat and had seen them creeping across the yard. They told us that she'd flapped her mat at them and cried out, "Go away—go away at once, boys! You are trespassing! Off you go!" Sophie and I had been on our back lawn that day, with Vicky hanging around as usual, when the boys came burst-ing through the fence and collapsed beside us, all hot and excited and guilty.

"Silly old bag!" gulped Ben. "We weren't doing any harm."

"She's really strange, isn't she," said Robbo. "All that straggly white hair and her stockings falling down. Do you think she's a witch?" He said this for Vicky's benefit, you could tell.

Ben sat up. "She might be! Gee—wouldn't it be ace to have a witch living next door!" He leered at Vicky. "Like the one in *Hansel and Gretel* who roasted up kids in the oven!"

Vicky's eyes were staring and huge. She was only just five then and believed in witches.

"Don't be pathetic, Ben!" scoffed Sophie. "There aren't any witches these days, not around here anyway. She wasn't riding a broomstick, was she?"

"No—she was waving a mat," grinned Ben. "It could

4

have been her magic carpet—she was probably getting ready for takeoff."

"I bet you two idiots just gave her a fright," I yawned, "and that made her hair stand on end and her stockings fall down."

"Well, I think they're prob'ly witches," wailed Vicky, staring at the hole in the fence that led into the dark forest, "and I wish they didn't live in there, so close. They make me scared."

Chapter 2

Everyone in the neighborhood said that *Featherbys* was a Disgrace and an Eyesore. I suppose that was because the neighbors all had perfect lawns and straight fences and clipped shrubs and huge plastic trash cans and boring concrete paths.

Featherbys was different. Its yard was a tangle of long weedy grass and scraps of litter. Many of the fence pickets were missing or dangling by one nail, like loose teeth, and the rest were swallowed up inside an ancient privet hedge. The top of the hedge bulged so far over the sidewalk that you almost had to walk in the gutter to get past, and in the late spring the white privet flowers made you sneeze—huge electrifying sneezes that tingled right down to your feet. The neighbors said the hedge was a Menace to Health, giving the whole street hay fever like that, and it should be dug out.

Dad came home from meetings of the Bottlebrush town council and said that there were often letters of complaint about *Featherbys* being a breeding ground for pests and vermin, not to mention privet pollen, and that it ought to be condemned, and all that stuff, and then Mum would say, "Those poor old dears, they just can't cope any more,"—meaning the two Miss Featherbys.

You couldn't see much of the old house from the street or over our back fence because the garden had run so wild. It was like looking into a dark, spooky jungle—without the wild animals, of course, although it was easy enough to imagine leopards crouching and pythons coiled in the branches overhead. Creepers had knitted themselves through the rotten lattices and into trees and over bushes, like shawls of ivy and curtains of morning glory, which flowered where they could reach the sun, but most of the garden was in deep shadow because of the huge trees above. They were twice as tall as any other trees in the suburb, and Mum said some of them must be a hundred years old.

According to Dad, the landscape architect chap at the town council complained that the giant trees at *Featherbys* spoiled the whole skyline. When we asked why, Dad explained that most landscape architects like trees to be all the same size—like the square black town council trash cans, I suppose.

Three quite modern houses backed onto *Featherbys*, and the four blocks together were like a rectangular island, with streets on four sides.

The Fontanas lived in the first modern house on the corner, with the Hugginses (that's us) in the middle, while the third house had just been bought by Mr. and Mrs. Pyle. When they moved in, the Pyles asked everyone, even kids, to call them Bartram and Sandra.

Bartram and Sandra explained to the neighbors that they were "into assets." "Assets, that's what it's all about," they kept saying. They never explained what they meant by "it," but I suppose they meant Life.

The Pyles each had two jobs and they already owned three cars and a boat, all of which filled the double garage and the driveway right up. They had assets instead of children, our parents told one another.

When the Pyles were not out making money at their jobs, or spending it on new assets, they were busy at home moving the three cars and the boat trailer in and out of the drive because the one they wanted to use always seemed to be at the back of the line. Next door, we played guessing games about what the Pyles' newest asset would be.

"Maybe they'll bring home a hot-air balloon," Ben guessed one evening.

Behind closed eyelids I imagined a huge red balloon floating dreamily above the Pyles' place. On one side was emblazoned a golden P catching the rays of the setting sun. P for PYLE. As the balloon dropped gently towards their back lawn, I pictured Bartram and Sandra drifting home from work in the wicker basket, gazing down at their assets and quaffing champagne from long glasses.

Perhaps this could be the start of a dazzling story of power and passion in a great business empire, something like *Dallas*....

Mum wrecked that idea. "And wouldn't they have fun landing the thing, with all those trees of Featherbys so close," she sniffed. My ideas for stories always seemed to end in ruins. I refocused my eyes to see Mum peering through the kitchen window, which overlooked the Pyles' driveway. Sandra was backing out the Mercedes, so that she could move the 4-wheel drive from in front of the Volvo, which she needed for her evening shopping trip. Sandra was wearing a deep mauve track suit and pink running shoes. She jogged everywhere by car.

"What happens if one asset runs into another asset and busts its radiator?" wondered Ben, joining Mum at the window.

"Insurance, that's what happens—if you're lucky," sighed Mum.

She was making a meat sauce, and the sizzle and smell of frying onions and tomatoes and spices had magnetized us all into the steamy kitchen. Mum doesn't engage in gourmet cookery every night because she works part-time at the Bottlebrush Hair Salon. (What a name! I reckon they should change it.) On some evenings, Mum works quite late and then it is up to me or Dad to feed the family. Dad is good at take-out—he's left it a bit late to become one of those Sensitive New Age Guys, the sort who can make Beef Stroganoff at five minutes' notice and clean up afterwards, but he does his best.

When we were a bit younger, Mum took time off during school holidays, but this would be the first time I was to be left in charge while Mum was out, now that I was old enough. I wasn't looking forward to it much. It would have been fairly okay without Vicky, but it was impossible to keep her going all day long without a screaming match.

Mum was a bit jittery about it, I could tell. As she stirred the meat sauce, off she went on the usual nag, "Now I hope you kids are going to find something sensible to do during vacation, especially when I'm at work during the day. I know the salon isn't far away and you can always ring me, but I like to know what you're up to when I'm over there. I won't have you hanging about the streets and getting into trouble."

"Okay Mum," I groaned. Mum always imagined that we'd be out there vandalizing phone booths and breaking into parking meters for funds, or checking around the local convenience stores or the Bottlebrush pool for gorgeous guys who would rush us off in fast, unroadworthy cars. Well, Mum didn't think too clearly—for one thing, the boys who hung around waiting to ambush girls were usually pimpled creeps on bikes, and no really gorgeous guy would want to rush Sophie and me off with three stupid kids in tow. Not a chance.

"Anyway," I said, "I'm going to sleep in every morning and take hours to get dressed and do my hair and face. I need a good rest from school—I'm a mental wreck."

"What will you be like in twelfth grade, if you're a mental wreck in the sixth?" asked Ben. That sort of problem interests Ben, who has a mathematical mind. He reads soccer statistics for fun. He could probably work out a growth rate—you know, multiplying my state of mental wreckage by 12/6 x 100, or something, to find out how far off the planet I'll be by the end of school.

I ignored him. In fourth grade what would *he* know about the strains of higher education?

Mum kept droning on, "Anyway, Jess, it wouldn't hurt you to give young Sophie a hand sometimes. If you want to know what being tired is, think of her. Since her mum died, she just about runs that house, as well as going to school and having to keep Robbo out of mischief. She's had to grow up so fast, poor kid."

"Yes, Mum, I *know*. I've already told her I'll help." Sophie was in the same boat as me, with Robbo to look after while her dad was at work. Having her next door would make all the difference—you know, someone on the same mental level to talk to when Vicky drove me up the wall. Besides, Sophie's dad had just bought them a new space-age washing machine, and we were looking forward to using it and working out all the different cycles.

I made the mistake of saying aloud, "Other people's housework is always more interesting than ours."

"Fancy that," said Mum, in a sarcastic voice.

Chapter 3

*N*ext day, my plans to sleep in and then spend hours in front of the bathroom mirror were ruined by Ben and Vicky, who wanted to be outside doing violent things in Mum's garden.

I rounded them up and we all went next door. The Fontanas' backyard was decorated around the edges with building supplies rather than beds of juicy young dahlias, so it was more suitable than ours for soccer and messing around. Mr. Fontana had learned to stack his spare windows behind the shed. Ben and Robbo were soon playing kickball, while Vicky rode her small bike up and down the concrete drive. This left me and Sophie free to check out the new washing machine. We read the instructions and then very skillfully operated two different cycles, one for woolens and one for "heavily soiled" work clothes, and soon the clothesline was flapping with jeans and school sweaters and Mr. Fontana's overalls and T-shirts and socks. It was only ten o'clock. Hours of childminding to go.

We wandered around to the front garden, and Sophie sprawled out on the lawn. "It's too gorgeous in the sun to do any more housework," she said.

I flopped down beside her. By now the boys were having a break from practicing and were on the front steps with their noses in a cricket magazine, reading batting averages or something deadly. It was that crazy time of year when they were switching their action from soccer to cricket. They didn't seem able to walk like normal human beings, but on every fifth step they'd do a sort of ballet routine either lining up and kicking for goal (winter) or playing a straight bat (summer). Just now it was spring, so they were in a muddle and doing both. At any moment, Ben would be rushing home to get his cricket stumps, I knew.

I rested one cheek on the grass. Down among the green blades and clover leaves in front of my nose I began to notice the tiny movements of insects. What were they all doing? I wondered, sleepily. Mr. Scrooby, our English teacher at school, said it was important to notice the smallest things. Would there be inspiration for a story down among the grass stalks where these beetle things were following endless trails and doing their housekeeping? I tried out the idea on Sophie.

"It's funny," I mumbled. "All these little bugs are plodding around down here and we never even think about them. I wonder what they're doing?"

So much for that idea—I should have saved my breath. "Mmm," was what Sophie said. She was lying on her back, with her eyes closed, looking more floppy than she usually did these days. I suppose Mum was right, Sophie had had to grow up fast. She wasn't nearly as bubbly as she used to be—she seemed to live inside herself, and I found it hard to reach her.

It worried me when I couldn't think what to say to Sophie after her mother died, because Mr. Scrooby had told me I have "a feeling for words." He said it in front of the whole class after reading out something I'd written about the ozone layer, and he became my favorite teacher after that. It made me wonder if I might even be a famous writer one day, although I knew I'd have to change my name first. Jess Huggins might do for a vet or a social worker, but it seemed a hopeless name for a writer—how ever could I write a romantic love story with a name like Huggins? Jessica was just possible if it had an elegant name stuck onto it, like Dalrymple or de Quincey. Jessica Dalrymple…Jessica de Quincey…would a name like that inspire me? As plain Jess Huggins I could never think of much to write about, although Mr. Scrooby said you have only to look around you to find all sorts of brilliant ideas to get you going. I didn't believe him. Nothing suitable for a story ever seemed to turn up in our street or our family.

As Sophie lay there, her thick black hair gleamed in the sun, that hair which made me a quivering heap of envy. All of the Hugginses are mousy. Just as well Mum works at the Bottlebrush Salon, because she has a few ideas about unmousifying hair. The Fontanas all have black hair because their family is Italian. Mrs. Fontana's hair had been the most beautiful of the lot, especially when she swept it up on top. I sighed into the grass and wondered for the thousandth time what it would be like to have no mother. I tried sometimes to imagine our family without Mum, but I couldn't think how to describe what it might feel like—like having an arm and a leg cut off, perhaps? No, there'd have to be a better way of putting it.

Lying there on the grass, I started to think of Mrs. Fontana's funeral eighteen months before and how awful it had been with everyone crying, and especially when

Mr. Fontana had started sobbing outside the church. I couldn't imagine Dad sobbing, but somehow *I* felt better after I'd had a good howl that day. But I just didn't know what to say to Sophie that would be any help—what can you say when someone like Mrs. Fontana dies, especially by accident? She was thirty-five, which wasn't exactly young, but it wasn't really old or even middle-aged when you thought of ancient people like the Featherbys, who were still alive. I imagined them skulking in their old house behind the trees. What did they do with themselves all day long?

By then Ben *had* rushed home to find his cricket stumps and Robbie was rehearsing his demon bowling action, while Vicky was still wound up in her endless bike ride. She was talking to herself and probably in a coma. I prodded Sophie.

"Hey, while the kids are busy, why don't we sneak into *Featherbys* for a bit? We haven't been in there for ages—and anyway we're probably getting skin cancer lying here in the UV rays, or I am, with my freaky skin." That was another thing about the Fontanas—to go with the black hair they had this olive skin that turned polished brown, no worries. I was on the verge of thinking it "wasn't fair," when I remembered Mrs. Fontana. Freaky skin and mousy hair didn't seem so important when you thought of her.

Sophie opened her eyes and stretched. "Oh, okay—we'll go and have a snoop if you want to." She didn't sound very interested.

"I don't suppose Vicky will want to come," I hoped, as I stood up. "She's scared of the place."

Vicky heard me as she rode by. "Yes, I am," she pouted. "Ben says they're witches, those old ladies. He says they'll put a spell on me."

"Ben's crazy," I told her, "but anyway you go on riding around here, and keep out of the way of that ball." It was only a tennis ball, but it could still knock your eye out, the way the boys slogged at it. "We'll be just through the fence and we won't be long."

Chapter 4

Sophie and I went around behind the shed to the back fence and squeezed through a gap into the shadows of the Featherby jungle. There was a smell of decay and damp leaf mold, and a chill fell on my sun-warm skin.

"There's some old wire netting collapsed under all this creeper," I whispered, "where the old chicken yards used to be, probably. Don't get tangled up in it—and watch out for spiders and slugs! Come over here where it's a bit clearer. This must have been a path once."

We crouched down and listened for a moment, then began to creep slowly forward, making little tunnels through the jungle. As we scrunched through the onion weed with its white bells, a kitcheny smell made our noses wrinkle up.

There were several old sheds behind the house, around a weedy yard. The boards on the sheds were streaked lime-green with moss, and the iron roofs were a faded red. A rusty wire was stretched across the yard, held up by a wooden prop. Two rags and a dingy petticoat were pegged on the wire.

"Your washing looks a lot better than theirs! I bet they don't have a space-age machine!" I hissed in Sophie's ear.

Sophie made a face. "No—and fancy not having a real clothesline! The sheets would all drag in the dirt if that prop thing fell over!"

We crept closer until we could see the house properly. Everything was silent except for blackbirds scratching in the leaf mold under the trees and, further away, the shouts of Ben and Robbo when a wicket fell. The back part of the old house was wooden, with a sagging verandah, and the rusty gutters and downspouts were as holey as sieves.

Suddenly Sophie breathed in my ear, "I'd love to see inside—just into one room!" It was great to see a gleam in Sophie's eyes for a change.

We listened carefully, then began tiptoeing across the yard towards the nearest window. The nerves were twangling in my stomach.

We were halfway across when the back wire door swung open with a sudden creak and Miss Violet Featherby appeared in a faded apron. She was carrying an old metal bucket and at first she didn't notice us. We both stood frozen in the middle of the yard. My stomach lurched. What were we going to *say*?

Miss Violet saw us just as she reached the verandah step. With a small shriek she dropped the bucket, clang! and reached out wildly for the rail to steady herself, but her toe caught in the bucket handle and she toppled down the step to the ground, where she lay, making little puffy gasps.

Sophie and I were still paralyzed, staring at her. "What'll we *do?*" hissed Sophie. "Do you think she's hurt herself?"

"Well, it wasn't our fault—she should've looked where she was going," I muttered crossly, "but I don't suppose we can leave her there. Oh, help." I don't know who I thought could help us—there was no one.

Before we were able to move, the door creaked again and banged open. Miss Alice was there, hobbling out with a stick! She was dressed in *black* and her face was wrinkled and grim. My eyes were probably as wide as Vicky's. Would this old hag capture us and shut us in a cage to fatten us up, like the witch in *Hansel and Gretel?*

How could I be such a dork at my age!

"What was that crash, Violet?" Miss Alice called. "What has happened?" She saw Violet lying on the ground, and then her eyes turned to us. "What are you two girls doing there? Where have you come from? And what have you done to my sister?" Her voice was hard and unfriendly. She was bigger and heavier than Violet, but rather stooped, and her white hair was carefully arranged in a bun. Violet's hair was in a bun, too, or more like a knot, but it looked as if she never had time to do it properly in front of a mirror.

Suddenly Sophie spoke up. "I'm Sophie Fontana— you know, from next door, at the back. We didn't mean any harm and I'm sorry your sister had a fright. She slipped down the step—I hope she's not hurt." Good old Sophie. Why couldn't I cope like that instead of being frozen into an icy pole by Miss Alice's cold stare?

"So, you're the Fontana girl, are you? Sophia, isn't it?" Alice stood there on the verandah studying Sophie and then she looked down again at Violet, who was now sitting on the step. "What's the matter with you, Violet? Are you hurt or not?" She didn't sound very sympathetic. In fact she seemed fairly horrible. All you could say in her favor so far was that she wasn't deaf and she didn't dribble.

"I'm not sure, I think it's my ankle," quavered Violet.

"Well, pull yourself together," said Alice rather severely. "You know we can't afford to have you falling down the stairs and spraining something."

Sophie gave me a nudge and we moved forward together.

"Let's see if we can help you up," offered Sophie, bending over the old lady. "Do you think you've sprained something?"

"I don't know." Violet was looking pale and shaky. Slowly she stretched out her leg and tried to move her foot, moaning a bit. "I don't think it's broken, but it's twisted. I shall have to rest it for a while."

"Let's help you. It's just as well we're here, really," I mumbled, trying to make the best of things. "Oh—and I'm Jess Huggins, from next door, too."

"Since you *are* here then," snapped Alice, "you can help my sister inside, and later on you can explain why you were both trespassing on our property."

I tried to forget that threat while Sophie and I gingerly held Violet's arms and helped her to stand. She was very skinny and I could feel her arm bones. It was easy to lift her up to the verandah and then support her as she hobbled inside. Her thick brown stockings were sagging again and her hair was all over the place. You could see her scalp through the thin gray wisps, and she could have done with a visit to the Bottlebrush Hair Salon right then, for a shampoo and the works.

Alice's stick came thumping along behind. "Take her in there, to the kitchen," she commanded, pointing to a doorway in a short passage.

Chapter 5

The kitchen was huge and dark, with just one window onto the verandah. We helped Violet to a chair and Sophie supported her foot on a low wooden stool and took off the shoe. The ankle looked rather swollen under the wrinkled stocking, although it was hard to see clearly in the dim light. The shabby brown blind on the window was only half raised.

"Do you think you should get the doctor?" asked Sophie.

"No, no, certainly not. We don't need anyone," snapped Alice. "It's not broken, is it, Violet." This wasn't a question, more like an announcement. If Mum had been there, she would have given Alice a lecture about osteoporosis and brittle bones and the importance of calcium in the female diet. When I thought of that I began to panic—at her age Violet *must* have busted something and it was all our fault!

But Violet shook her head timidly. "No, Alice. Just twisted, probably, but I don't think I can walk on it for a while yet."

"What about a bandage?" I suggested. "It needs some support." I'd been to First Aid classes at school and ankle-strapping was one of my top skills, and I knew about not bandaging too tight in case of cutting off the blood supply to the whole foot. Toes might drop off if you do that, but not straightaway, of course.

"Have we any bandages, Violet?" asked Alice.

"Perhaps there's something in that drawer over there—the middle one."

Violet pointed towards an enormous dresser, which I hadn't noticed in the gloom because I'd been busy dealing with an emergency. Its shelves were cluttered with plates and dangling cups, jars, old rubber gloves, rusty scissors, tattered recipe books, pieces of string, two mouse-traps, and other junk.

Sophie opened the drawer and rummaged through a muddle of cloths and tea towels. At the bottom she found some old sheeting. "Will this do? Can I tear it?"

Violet nodded. "Yes, yes—that will do."

Sophie tore the linen into long strips, and I began to wind them crisscross round Violet's ankle.

"It would be better without the stocking," I told her. "Would you be able to take it off?"

Violet gasped. I suppose I should have realized she'd be embarrassed to death at her age, in front of kids like us, but in the end she said, "Oh, dear me—yes, I suppose it would be better."

She fumbled with her stocking, which (I saw from the corner of my eye) was held up by an elastic garter just above her knee. Sophie and I gazed tactfully around the room. All the kitchens I know are pretty fancy, gleaming with laminated benches and stainless steel, but there was nothing like that here. The big table was wooden, and the stained porcelain sink in the corner had a rickety water heater on the wall above. There was a gas stove on legs, like something in a cartoon, but the thing I couldn't take my eyes off (once I'd seen it) was an enormous black wood-burning range. It was out...and just as well, I thought, remembering the oven in *Hansel and Gretel*. Alice was standing in front of it leaning on her stick and frowning.

"There," sighed Violet, sinking back. She had pulled her skirt down as low as possible over her bare leg. The skin I could see was as white as chalk and not quite human. I suppose it had never seen the sun. Her foot was thin and bony, with round yellow corns on several toes. Ugh! Dead white skin and yellow corns would have to be added to the Geriatric List.

I felt a bit squeamish as I began again to bandage the ankle, but then I thought that nurses and ambulance men do much more horrible things all day long, like picking up fingers that have been chopped off or mopping up liters of blood or something even *worse*. Was this really me strapping up Miss Violet Featherby's skinny foot, with its yellow corns and blue veins? Sophie had found a safety pin on the dresser to fasten the bandage with.

Violet carefully waggled her strapped-up foot and for the first time looked more cheerful. "Oh, that feels *much* better. Thank you, girls."

Alice thumped her stick on the floor. "There's a spare walking stick in the hall that you can use to help you move around, Violet," she said. "And now, young ladies, you can explain how you happened to be in our yard, trespassing."

My heart lurched against my ribs—I'd hoped Alice would forget about the trespassing, but she didn't seem to be that sort of person. More like a female dragon, really, breathing fire and smoke...

"Alice," began Violet. "Don't you think...?"

"Be quiet, Violet. Let them explain themselves."

Sophie and I looked sideways at each other, then we both started to chatter like idiots.

"We just wanted to see the house close up," faltered Sophie. "You can't see it from the street."

"It's so old," I gabbled. "It's quite different from all the other houses around here...sort of mysterious and interesting...."

Alice seemed to unstiffen a little and she almost allowed herself a tiny smile. Heavens! What had I said to soften her up? If she'd smiled more she could have been quite nice looking, I decided. She was standing there proudly. "Featherbys have always lived here, you know. When Grandfather died, my father and mother came to live here—we were all born here."

"Do you mean you've *always* lived in this house?" gaped Sophie.

"Yes, of course—but when we were young, there were very few other houses close by. Bottlebrush was just a crossroads with a store and a church and some outlying farms. We owned all the land hereabouts and it was real countryside...so beautiful. Do you remember, Violet, we kept our ponies in the field just beyond where these girls live now."

"Of course I remember, Alice, and the stables were on one of those new blocks—yes, the one where you live," she said to Sophie, "and the orchard covered the others."

I stared through the window towards our houses and pictured rows of fruit trees, and beyond them wide paddocks and sheep grazing and bushland. There would once have been spreading gums with magpies or cockatoos in their top branches, but all that had now been gobbled up by yards and cement gutters and service stations. I looked around the old kitchen and tried to fill it with a proper family, or with servants perhaps, and baskets of fruit being brought in from the orchard to be made into cauldrons of jam and chutney on the big black stove. The hardest thing to imagine was these two old ladies as little girls, riding their ponies back to the stables to be unsaddled and groomed.

Sophie was also peering through the window towards her place, where the stables had been, although she couldn't see that far because of the trees and creepers. Suddenly she jumped. "Oh heavens, Jess! The kids! We're supposed to be keeping an eye on the boys and Jess's little sister while our parents are at work," she explained to the Featherbys. "They'll wonder what's happened—we've been away for ages!"

"You must be off then," said Alice, rapping her stick on the floor.

We started to go but as we were leaving Sophie said shyly, "Would you mind if we came again tomorrow, just to see if anything needs doing while Miss Violet's ankle is getting better? She shouldn't really be walking on it." Sophie was amazingly brave. I wouldn't have dared to ask.

Violet brightened up. "Oh—that would be nice. Perhaps a little milk from the shop, for our tea—and by then we might need some firewood brought in for the stove— you know, just a few little things like that. It *would* be kind—such a help." She glanced nervously at her sister.

Alice began to fidget with her stick. "Well, all right— just while Violet is recovering. But that doesn't mean that we *need* help, you know. There's no call to say anything about Violet's silly accident, do you understand? We don't want any fuss."

I couldn't imagine why the old dragon was so touchy, but at least she didn't want to imprison us or fatten us up for the oven. We mumbled our goodbyes and dashed outside, through the shadowy wilderness and the hole in the fence into the Fontanas' sunny backyard. It was like another world.

Vicky, Ben, and Robbo stood around, staring. "Where've you *been*?" whimpered Vicky. "We thought the witches had got you!"

Sophie and I fled around to the front lawn and collapsed there, giggling and gasping—the way you do after an ordeal, like being summoned to see the principal at school. The kids trailed after us.

"What's the matter? Why are you acting so weird?" Ben wanted to know. "What happened?"

Sophie sat up at last. "We met the Miss Featherbys."

"Well…what *happened*?"

"We're not supposed to say." She started giggling again.

"What do you mean? Did they put a spell on you?" breathed Vicky.

"Of course not!" I scoffed. "We're just not supposed to talk about it."

The boys were desperate. "Can't you tell *us*? It will be a secret—just the four of us."

"And me!" wailed Vicky. "Five of us."

Sophie and I made faces while we thought about it. It was good fun stringing the kids along like that, but Sophie weakened before I did.

"Actually, Jess," she said, "the kids could be quite useful. Miss Violet said something about firewood, didn't she?"

"Did she? Yes, maybe she did. Well…okay," I agreed, "but you three have got to promise not to say anything to anyone just yet."

So we told them all about it, right up to fastening the safety pin in Violet's bandage and Alice accusing us of trespassing, and then Robbo said, "It must have been really *bad* when she fell down the steps, but why does it have to be a secret? We're always falling over and nobody minds."

"We don't know why," Sophie frowned. "Miss Alice seemed really cross with Miss Violet for falling over. She's frightfully bossy, isn't she?"

"I'll say!—she orders everyone around," I said, "but d'you know what I think? I think she's really scared she'll be left on her own if something happens to Miss Violet. I bet it's Violet who does everything—you know, the cooking and all that, and old Alice wouldn't be able to cope on her own. Violet's like her slave."

"I know—that's why I asked if we could go back tomorrow," said Sophie.

"Are you going *back*?" Vicky gasped.

"Yes, we're allowed to. Sophie asked if we could, just to help with a few things so that old Bossyboots won't have poor Miss Violet hopping around on her sore ankle," I explained. "You were pretty cool!" I told Sophie.

Sophie collapsed again. "I was scared to bits, especially after all that stuff about trespassing. But I'm sorry for Miss Violet—I think she's quite nice, really—and I'd love to see more inside the house."

"Me, too. You ought to see the kitchen, kids. No dishwasher or microwave or anything like that, and I think

they sometimes light a wood fire in the stove for cooking."

"Cool! Can we come with you tomorrow?" asked Ben.

"Well...I suppose it'd be all right...as long as you behave properly, *if* you know how. But you'll have to stay
outside until we explain that you've come to help. They're
very nervous."

Chapter 6

Next morning after all the parents had gone to work, Sophie and I flew around doing the basic chores, and we sent the boys to the shop for Violet's carton of milk and some bread. I hunted in the bathroom cupboard until I found a clean cloth bandage, and Sophie whipped up a quick orange cake to take next door. She was getting to be a good cook. We'd all been careful to say nothing to our parents about the Featherbys—even Vicky had held her tongue, with me and Ben ready to pounce on her.

In the morning Vicky said, "I'll come through the hole with you, but I think I'll just wait near the fence."

"All right," I agreed. "You can make yourself a little nest there. Now," I said, when everyone was ready, "do you all look clean and decent?"

"Why do we need to look special?" Robbo grumbled. "Old Violet's stockings are always falling down, so she probably wouldn't notice."

"But Miss Alice would." I retied the tartan hair ribbons on Vicky's mousy plaits. "Miss Alice is very picky—but if we all look respectable and behave politely she's more likely to let us visit again."

"What for?" cried Vicky. "I don't even want to go once!"

"Well—it's such an amazing place. Wait till you see inside!" answered Sophie. "Oh, we forgot to tell you that when they were kids the Featherbys used to keep ponies out there just in front of our places. It used to be paddocks and real country. Our house is on top of where their stables were."

"Fancy them ever being kids!" Ben snorted. "It must have been back in the Middle Ages."

"Ha, ha, Ben Huggins. Just mind what you say if you don't want to get put in the oven! Okay. Are we all ready? Let's go."

Sophie and I led the way, carrying the food and the milk, and climbed carefully through the fence, followed by the others. Vicky shivered as she peered about the dark old garden with its green creeper caves and the ghostly tunnels Sophie and I had made the day before. Spots of pale sunlight flickered through the leaves and here and there dead branches stuck through the green curtains like bones. It was damp and cold.

"I don't want to stay here by myself," whimpered Vicky. I knew she wouldn't. "I'll come a bit further so that I can see where you are—somewhere that's not so dark."

We pushed our way through the creepers to the over-grown path. The boys began to fool about, crawling along dark trails and growling like wild animals. "Watch out!" hissed Ben, pouncing on Vicky from behind a bush. "There's a jaguar in that tree, ready to spring!"

Vicky wailed and grabbed my free hand. "Shut up, Ben," I snapped, "and for goodness sake stay with us! Don't ruin everything now, dork brain."

We reached the open yard. "You three sit here, by this shed," ordered Sophie. "Jess and I will go inside and see what's happening and ask if you can do something to help. But don't do *anything* until we come back."

Ben, Robbo, and Vicky sat down nervously on an old bench outside the shed, while we went to the door and knocked.

"Who is it?" called Violet's voice, faintly.

"It's us—Sophie and Jess."

"Oh! Come in, girls—into the kitchen."

We found Violet sitting on the same chair with her bandaged foot on the stool.

"How's your ankle?" Sophie asked her. "You haven't been there all night, have you?" Sophie smiled, but she was only half joking.

"Goodness no, I've been to bed, but I thought I'd better get my sister some breakfast this morning. She was very tired after all yesterday's fuss and bother, so she's staying in bed for a while."

I shot Sophie an "I-told-you-so" look. I knew I'd been right—Violet was a slave!

"But how's your foot?" repeated Sophie, a bit snappishly. I suppose like me she was thinking of Violet struggling with a tray and a walking stick so that the dragon lady could have breakfast in bed.

"The ankle's a little better I think, but I can't stand on it for long."

"I've brought you a cloth bandage," I told her, digging it out of my pocket. "It's more stretchy than that old linen. Would you like me to change it for you?"

"That's very kind of you, Jess." Violet settled back in her chair and began to roll her stocking down. She'd gotten used to us now.

"Here's the milk, too, and some bread," said Sophie, "and I've made you an orange cake. Where shall we put them?"

"How delicious! What good girls you are. It's such a nuisance that milk is no longer delivered. If you go through that doorway, you'll find the pantry and you can put the things in there."

We found ourselves in a dark, narrow room lined with shelves. At one end sat an old refrigerator with curved corners. We put the food into it and heaved shut the heavy door. There wasn't much else in the fridge, except thick frost and some margarine, and there were just a few cans of food on the pantry shelves and a lot of empty jars. I wondered what the Featherbys would be eating for dinner.

Then I unwrapped Violet's ankle. It was less swollen but now the white skin was mottled with yellow and purple bruises. I really loved practicing my ankle-strapping skills, and this time I didn't feel any squeams at all.

"You shouldn't walk on it," Sophie warned her. "It'll take much longer to get better if you do."

"I know, but there are things to be done."

"Well, let us help you. That's why we've come…and our brothers are waiting outside to see if there's something they can do, like getting firewood. We hope you don't mind them coming in, too."

"Well, no—I expect it will be all right. It's just that my sister is nervous of intruders."

No wonder they were nervous, in that dark, lonely, overgrown house.

I called Ben and Robbo to come. Vicky stayed glued to the bench. The boys shuffled in, looking at the floor.

"This is Ben and that one's Robbo," Sophie pointed.

"Good morning, boys. I do believe we've met before—in the yard, wasn't it?" There was a tiny smile on Violet's face, but the boys were too embarrassed to notice. They mumbled their hellos and just stood there like blobs. Then Ben saw the old black stove.

"Can you really use that for cooking things on?" he asked.

"Oh, I often do," Violet answered. "It makes the room much cozier, especially in winter, but it's gone out now and I haven't been able to fetch more firewood."

"We'll get you some," offered Robbo, "and would we be allowed to light the fire in the stove, too, if you tell us how?"

"Well…if you're careful and do what I say," agreed Violet. "The woodshed is across the yard, for bigger logs, and you can collect kindling around the garden and snap it into small pieces."

"While you're out there," I told them, "make sure that Vicky is okay."

"Vicky?" asked Violet, anxiously.

"You know, my little sister. She's only five and she's scared of coming in, so she's waiting by the shed."

"Oh, then she might help to collect the kindling and bring it in," suggested Violet. "I used to like doing that when I was five."

I pushed the boys towards the back door before Ben mentioned the Middle Ages again, and then I came back to Sophie and the old lady.

"Those boys remind me so much of my brother," sighed Violet. "He used to bring in the firewood at their age. He didn't have to, of course—one of the gardeners would have done it—but Arthur loved chopping the wood."

"I didn't know you had a brother," said Sophie.

"We haven't any more. He went away to the war when he was twenty-three and he didn't come back. He was killed in action in North Africa."

Once again I couldn't think what to say—my mouth just dried up. North Africa seemed a peculiar place for an Australian to be fighting a war in, and it must have been ages ago if he was only twenty-three. It seemed silly to say I was sorry now, after so long. I did manage to ask, "Which war was it?"

"The Second World War, dear—the big one. Arthur died in 1942."

Fifty years ago!

Then Sophie asked, "Did you have any more brothers?"

"No. Arthur was the only one. He was the youngest of us. We had another sister, too, who married. She also died quite young, when her little boy was nine."

Suddenly Sophie said, "My mum died last year, in a car accident."

Violet looked at her. "I know. She was far too young. You must miss her very badly."

I was beginning to like Miss Violet—we hardly knew her, but here she was already talking about important things like dying. Sophie must have felt the same about her, because she went on about her mother.

"I'm getting used to Mum not being around, I s'pose," she said, "but it's still like having an empty black space in the house. And inside me, too. It's always there somewhere—I can sort of *feel* it." She clutched her arms around her chest. Sophie's "empty black space" sounded a much better description than my idea of having an arm and a leg cut off, but Sophie really *knew* what it felt like to have no mother—I guess that made the difference. I'd never heard Sophie talk like that since the funeral, and here she was saying these things to an old lady she hardly knew.

Violet was nodding. "Yes—a black space. What a good way of putting it. Of course we all have to die sometime, and I don't mind about it very much at my age, but it's such a waste to die young like your mother, and my brother and sister. But your mother would be very proud of the way you are looking after things, I'm sure. That's just what she'd want."

"It's great to have Jess and the Hugginses next door," said Sophie. I felt myself flush a bit, but I *loved* hearing her say that because it meant that she wanted to have me around even though I didn't know what to say about her mum.

"Yes, it's wonderful to have a good friend," said Violet, "and I hope you and I can be friends, too." She patted Sophie's hand and smiled at me. I wondered if Violet had any friends left, stuck away there in the jungle.

The back door creaked and slammed as the kids marched in carrying armfuls of firewood and sticks. Vicky, almost hidden behind a bundle of kindling, staggered as far as the doorway and stopped. Violet smiled at her but said nothing.

"There's not much wood left in the shed," Robbo reported. "We had to find dead branches and things in the garden and break them up."

"I tried to use the ax," said Ben. "I wasn't much good at it, but I'm going to practice. I wish we had a fireplace at home."

"How do we light the stove?" asked Robbo, dumping his load on the hearth.

Violet told them how to rake the ashes through the grate into the ashpan below and how to lay the fire, with paper and chips, in the narrow firebox. She explained about opening the flue for a good draft to fan the flames until the fire was going well.

They did what she told them and then Ben struck a match and held it to the paper. Soon the flames were roaring back towards the flue, and we all gathered around, staring. Vicky, still clutching her bundle of sticks, quietly edged up to join us.

"Keep feeding in more chips—don't let it die down," cried Violet, "and as the coals build up, put on some bigger pieces."

Before long, there were hot coals, and the boys gingerly poked in several larger lumps of wood.

"Good! That's just right, boys. Now, shut the little door and close up the flue a bit so that all the heat doesn't go up the chimney. Next thing is to fill the kettles and put them on top."

Sophie and I filled the two black kettles from the tap over the sink and heaved them onto the range.

"They won't take too long if you put them in the middle over the flames," said Violet. "Once they boil, you can move them to the sides, where they'll just simmer."

"Isn't it clever!" Sophie was gazing at the old stove. "Except that you've got to remember to feed it with wood. What are the other doors for?"

"The two big ones on either side are ovens, and the little ones below them are plate warmers. You can warm your shoes or your feet in there, too, in the winter."

I started tidying up the hearth with a brush and pan. Robbo stacked the firewood into a big woodbox at one side, and Vicky spoke at last.

"What'll I do with my bundle?"

"Put it in the other box, dear, on this side. Then it will be all ready for next time the stove needs lighting," said Violet, "and that will be such a help to me." That was another thing about Violet—she'd noticed Vicky at the door, but she hadn't gushed all over her and frightened her into a panic. By now, Vicky had decided that Violet wasn't a witch.

"I want to light the match next time," said Vicky, solemnly.

The gloomy old kitchen had come to life and the kettles began to sing.

"I think we'll have a cup of tea," decided Violet.

Chapter 7

While we were setting cups and saucers on the table, there was a sudden loud knocking at the back door and a man's voice called, "Is anyone there? Are you at home, Aunt Violet?"

Violet jumped slightly and said, "Oh dear." She pulled her chair closer in and pushed her bandaged foot under the table. "It's our nephew, Mervyn. Mr. Bottomley."

"Should I tell him to come in?" I asked her, hoping that stupid Ben wouldn't snort. Ben collected names like "Bottomley."

"Yes, please, Jess, you'd better."

When I opened the back door, a red-faced man stood there staring at me.

"Who the devil are you?" said the man, rudely. "What are you doing here?"

"I live next door—over the back way," I replied, as politely as I could, although I felt like sticking my tongue out at him. He was one of those prickly people who bring you out in a rash. "We're helping Miss Violet with a few jobs."

"Huh! Are you just." Mervyn Bottomley strode towards the kitchen and barged through the door. He looked suspiciously at the morning tea party round the table.

"Well—this is a nice little picnic!" Mervyn Bottomley didn't sound very friendly. "What's going on, Aunt Vi? This kid says they're helping you with jobs. It looks more to me as if they're eating you out of house and home."

"Nonsense, Mervyn." Violet turned to face him. "They have been helping with the firewood and the stove, and now we're just having a pick-me-up. In any case, Sophia brought the cake—she made it herself."

The kids were now sitting closely around Violet, and Sophie was pouring the tea from a blue and white pot. It had a Chinese pattern on it.

Mervyn's eyes were flicking about. "Why do you need all these helpers? You and Aunt Alice are always saying you can manage on your own."

I butted in, quickly, "It's just that we're all on school break and we're looking for things to do. There's nothing wrong with that, is there?" I could tell that Violet was trying to keep her bandaged ankle out of sight.

"I'm allowed to light the fire next time," Vicky told him.

Sophie handed Mr. Pig Bottomley a cup of tea, although I wouldn't have. He grunted and began to slurp it down. "Well, maybe when the vacation is over and you kids aren't here to help any more, these aunties of mine will start to realize that they can't cope as well as they thought. I'm always at them to leave this place and move to an apartment, you know." He gulped some more tea and turned his red face again to Violet. "You're crazy to go on living here...or just plain stubborn."

Thumps in the passage announced the arrival of Alice, who must have just finished dressing. She was wearing a sort of plum-colored frock instead of black, but she looked just as dragonish as the day before and I could feel Vicky cowering behind my knees.

"Oh, so it's you, Mervyn—I wondered whose voices I could hear," said the old lady. "And the children again, too—even more of them! Well, what have you come for, Mervyn?"

Mr. Bottomley bristled. "I'm allowed to call, I hope, to see if my aunts are okay? I was passing, as it happens, and I wanted you to know that I've seen a decent little unit for sale about four streets from here. It would be just right for you two."

Alice thumped the floor with her stick. "I might have guessed! How often do I have to tell you that Violet and I are perfectly content here and that we have no intention of moving just yet. And in any case, we are not going to discuss our private matters before all these children. You'd better come with me, Mervyn, to the front room. Come!"

Mervyn plonked down the cup and followed Alice out of the kitchen. There was a short silence and then Vicky said, "I don't like that man."

"Shush, Vick!" I nearly shriveled up—she was so embarrassing! Next thing she'd be calling out that Miss Alice was a witch!

"It's all right, Jess," Violet sighed. "I understand how the child feels. But I think you must realize that Mervyn hasn't had a very happy life."

Sophie remembered what Violet had told us before. "Is he the one who was nine years old when your sister died?" she asked.

"He's the one, yes."

How could Mervyn Bottomley ever have been a boy of nine? He looked about fifty now, red-faced and cross.

Voices were raised in another part of the house. Mr. Bottomley was talking very loudly, almost shouting. We could hear him telling his Aunt Alice that *Featherbys* was a disgrace to the neighborhood, with the house falling down and the yard turning to jungle.

Ben said to Violet, "If Mr. Bottomley is your nephew, why doesn't he come and help you to fix things up a bit?"

"He doesn't seem to have the time," answered Violet. She looked tired and sad. "You'd think he'd be more interested—I suppose he will live here in the end."

We all stared at her.

"Mr. Bottomley will? What do you mean?" said Robbo.

"Well, when Alice and I have gone, he'll be the only one of the family left. The house will be his."

Sophie and I looked at one another. This was an awful piece of news. A real shocker. We didn't want beastly Mervyn Bottomley as a neighbor, the owner of *Featherbys*. I was not ready to think of *Featherbys* without Miss Violet and Miss Alice, or to think of *them* as old ladies who could soon die. We'd only just met them.

"Mr. Bottomley doesn't even seem to *like* the place," Sophie muttered to me.

In the distance, the voices had stopped and a door banged.

"He's gone," said Violet. "That was the front door. Alice must have sent him off."

Slowly Alice came thumping back down the passage.

She appeared in the doorway, white-faced, and stared at her sister.

"It's as we feared—Mervyn wants to sell the place," she said, stonily. "As soon as we're dead and gone...or sooner, if he can move us out!" She noticed us all standing around. "You young people must go now. Off with you! My sister and I need to talk."

Chapter 8

The next Saturday the Pyles had an outdoor lunch party. *Alfresco* they called it.

Bartram shut the boat and the 4-wheel drive in the double garage and moved the Volvo and the Mercedes out of the driveway and parked them in the street. They arranged white tables and striped beach umbrellas on the paved area around the new electric barbecue. Sandra had jazzed up two small potted cypresses with big pink bows and there were matching pink napkins on the tables. Gee! this had once been the Featherbys' orchard, trees loaded with apples and cherries, and red windfalls lying in the thick grass. Now it was concrete paving and pink bows.

Ben, as usual, was the first to notice what was happening and rushed to bring Robbo in for the sideshow. There were some small knotholes in the boards of our side fence, and the boys had a dog's-eye view of the Pyles' back garden through these. They were camouflaged by small bushes on both sides of the fence.

There wasn't much to see at first as most of the party preparations were happening inside the Pyles' house, and the boys kept coming back into our kitchen to get cookies to keep themselves alive. At about midday Ben hurtled in for more supplies.

"The show's just starting," he told me. "Boy, you ought to see Sandra!"

I'd grown out of spying on the neighbors through holes in the fence, but this was the Pyles' first party and I thought I should check it out as it might provide me with useful material about late twentieth century society. Mr. Scrooby was always roaring at us to be Observant about the world around us. I made myself a honey and peanut butter sandwich and climbed in under the bushes with the boys. There were plenty of spare knotholes, and I stuck my eye to one just in time to see Sandra appearing in a designer outfit of jeans and white T-shirt, with Italian sandals that clonked on the cement as she walked. Around her neck were twined about twenty gold chains and strings of beads, huge gold crescent earrings dangled from her ears, and her arms and fingers were loaded with bracelets and chunky rings.

"See what I mean?" hissed Ben. "Sort of gold-plated." Mum said later that you have to have two jobs and no kids to be able to dress like that. Mum had been spying through the kitchen window.

I rather hoped that Sandra in her clonky heels would sprain her ankle too, like Violet, so that I could rush to the rescue with more bandages and my First Aid skills and perhaps be rewarded with champagne to drink—but she didn't.

Then Bartram came out carrying the barbecue tools. Over his skin-tight black jeans he wore a long apron with a drunk-looking ostrich on it. Bartram also had on a new hat and shades.

"What a geek!" snorted Robbo, under his breath.

The guests began to drive up. Most of them seemed

to be "into assets," too, judging by the large, shiny cars that were gradually clogging up the street on both sides. We kept our eyes rammed to the fence holes as the guests strolled up the drive. They all looked about the same age as Bartram and Sandra—there were no old people or children.

"Hello, *darlings!* What a fabulous outdoor living area!" shrieked the women.

"G'day mate!" the men shouted to one another, shaking hands and slapping backs.

Bartram began pouring champagne and beer while Sandra clonked about among her guests carrying a huge platter of nibble food, and the babble of voices was pierced by high shrieks of laughter and the chink of glass. Bartram had turned on the barbecue and was now flourishing his cooking tools and greasing the grill. We all began to feel gapingly hungry, so Ben raced inside again and came back with cheese crackers and a box of raisins, which were pretty pathetic when the smell of barbecue was oozing through the knotholes and straight up our nostrils.

"Look who's just arrived!" hissed Robbo, as Ben crept back under the bush. "It's old Bott from next door!"

"Old who?" I asked.

"That Mr. Bottomley—you know, from *Featherbys.* Their nephew!"

"Him!" Ben peered through the hole. "Gee, yes—imagine him knowing the Pyles!"

The barbecue was fairly close to the fence and we could watch Bartram in his ostrich apron, his face red and perspiring under the bush hat as he joggled the steaks and sizzled the shrimp. The luscious smell was almost too much for Ben and Robbo to bear. They had finished the cheese crackers and were near the bottom of the raisin box. My stomach was aching too. I hoped Mum was inside slaving over a hot gourmet lunch for us all.

Mervyn Bottomley, holding his glass of beer, came strolling over to the barbecue.

"Nice place you have here, Bart," he remarked. "High class."

"Thanks, Merv. Yes, we like it," glowed Bartram, flipping a shrimp. "We need more space though, you know—we'd like a pool and more off-street parking and so forth. It's a damned nuisance having to leave some of the vehicles in the drive."

"Yeah, must be," agreed Mervyn, "and there wouldn't be much room for a pool up at the back there. Too close to all those huge trees next door, anyway—they'd mess it up. Real eyesore, aren't they." Mervyn glowered up at the forest of Featherby trees towering above.

"You're not wrong, Merv," groaned Bartram. "That place is a bloody disgrace, and I wouldn't mind betting there are rats. Two old dears live there, I'm told. The house is over on the other side of the property. Obviously they can't cope any more."

"Obviously," said Mervyn, taking a casual swill of beer. "It just so happens I know them, and, well...I've tried to persuade them to move into a unit, but you know how pig-headed old women can be. They've gone a bit gaga, I reckon. Can't see what's best for themselves, silly old cows."

Ben and Robbo stared at me, but I signaled them to shut up. Mervyn Bottomley was still talking.

"Come to think of it, if *you* need more space," he

said to Bartram, "you could be doing the old girls a favor by buying a bit of their land—down this end, backing onto your block. That'd give you a really decent area for your pool and another garage, with plenty of room to turn and a separate entrance from the side street. You ought to think about it. It'd be a great investment, too. First-rate."

The steak began to smoke and burn while Bartram thought about it. "That's quite a proposition, Merv," he said, "but they probably don't want to sell. Wouldn't they have done so by now?"

"Huh! I don't think they know what they want," sniffed Mervyn, "but it ought to be easy enough to persuade them. At their age they should be a pushover."

Bartram, cooking tongs poised in midair, gazed towards the Featherbys' land. I bet in his mind's eye he was planning on a four-car garage, with extra room for the boat, and a kidney-shaped blue pool, with spa, surrounded by green cement. Probably Sandra would like a couple of those large tropical palms at the poolside, the ones that look dead for the first year or two because they've been dug up and carted to the other end of the country and a different climate. Still, Bartram would probably reckon them a great improvement on the Featherbys' jungle.

He jumped and swore as he noticed black smoke rising from the hissing steak, and hastily he began to call "Come and *ged*-it!" to his guests. Behind the fence we sniggered—the meat didn't smell half so yum any more. Then we crawled away to a quiet corner of our back lawn.

"Did you hear *that*!" exploded Robbo.

"Course I heard it—Bott is trying to sell *Featherbys*, and without even asking the old girls. What's he up to?" asked Ben.

"I don't know. He didn't even let on that they were his aunts."

"He's a real rat," Robbo growled. "What'll we do?"

"Let's tell Sophie first," I decided. "Come on."

Sophie was in her kitchen getting some lunch. Mr. Fontana was out in the shed cleaning his tools.

When we'd brought Sophie up to the minute with the grapevine news, Ben asked, "Do you think we should let the Featherbys know?"

"I suppose we ought to warn them," I said, "in case the Pyles suddenly spring it on them. They might get muddled and do something silly. I've heard of old ladies signing things without knowing what they're doing."

"Yes, we'd better tell them—but don't mention Mr. Bottomley yet," warned Sophie. "It'll only upset Violet and Alice even more if they know it's *his* idea."

Chapter 9

*L*ater that day, the four of us lined up at the Featherbys' back door. We found Violet in the kitchen, as usual. She was poking the stove, so the boys said they would empty the ashes and bring in another load of wood.

"Where's little Vicky today?" asked Violet.

"She's gone to a birthday party," I explained. "But we've got something to tell you—and we think Miss Alice ought to hear it, too. It's about our new neighbors, the Pyles."

"Goodness, whatever have they got to do with us?" asked Violet. "We don't even know them."

"Well, you just might meet them quite soon," said Sophie.

"Really? Why do you think that? Oh, thank you, boys—just put it in the usual place, that's such a help!" Ben and Robbo stacked their firewood in the woodbox, and then Violet said, "I think Alice is in the front room, so we'd better go in there, if you think it's important—whatever you have to tell us."

I elbowed Sophie. Here was our chance to see more of the old house!

Violet was leaning on a walking stick, and she led us slowly along the dim central passage towards the front. Several rooms opened off each side of the passage, but most of the doors were shut except for one into a gloomy room with a big table in it. The table was covered with a heavy brown fringed cloth, and I guessed this must be the dining room. Did the old ladies ever sit at either end of the table for dinner? The passage had dark, rather creaky floorboards with a carpet strip down the middle, and at the front of the house it widened into an entrance hall. There were narrow colored windows framing the front door, and they reflected blue and crimson shimmers onto a dusty side table, while opposite stood a tall hatstand holding a cluster of walking sticks and two black umbrellas, with some faded straw hats on the pegs. I kept an eye on Ben in case he scrawled *Clean me* in the dust as he sometimes did on cars parked in the street. There was a musty mothball smell and a feeling of chill.

Violet hobbled through a doorway off the hall calling, "Are you there, Alice? We have a deputation to see us."

"What ever do you mean, Violet?" we heard Alice reply in a snappy sort of voice.

"It's all right, Miss Featherby," said Sophie, following Violet into the room. "It's only us, but we have something important to tell you both."

"Is that so?" Alice was sitting in a high-backed chair near the window, with a small rug over her knees. The room had heavy curtains, and it was crowded with more large furniture. In the gloom I noticed many photographs in dull silver frames, including several of a young man in uniform. I guessed he must have been Arthur Featherby, the brother who was killed in the war. Over the mantelpiece hung a portrait of a whiskery man who looked rather severe, like Miss Alice. Perhaps he was her grandfather, the one who had built the house. I wished we could ask questions.

"Well, what is it, child?" Alice was impatient.

"The boys can tell you," said Sophie.

The old ladies turned to stare at the boys. Robbo nudged Ben, who stood on one leg. "Well," croaked Ben, "there are new neighbors next to us, Mr. and Mrs. Pyle...and, um, we think they might want to buy some of your land, the bit down at the end behind their place."

"Oh, goodness," gasped Violet.

Alice frowned at Ben. "And how do you know this?" she asked.

"Well—the Pyles were having a sort of party, a barbecue, and we just heard them talking over the fence...they were talking quite loudly and we couldn't help hearing. Mr. Pyle was moaning away about not having enough room for their cars and...someone suggested they ought to buy some of your land for more parking space."

"For more parking space?" repeated Alice, coldly. "Do you mean they want to turn *our* garden into a garage?"

"They've got three cars and a boat on a trailer," Robbo tried to explain. "There isn't really room for them all on their block."

"Why ever do they need so many?" asked Violet.

"Well, they use two of them to get to work," said Ben, "and the 4-wheel drive pulls the boat trailer. Anyway, the Pyles call them assets."

"Assets!" snapped Alice. "Assets!" She grasped her stick and slowly stood up. "Come with me. I'll show you assets!"

"Whatever are you doing, Alice?" quavered Violet, following her into the hall.

"I'm going to show these young people around the garden," said Alice as she unchained the front door. "You'd better stay here, Violet, and rest your ankle."

"Oh, dear—well, I suppose I'll have to. But you haven't been out there for a long time, Alice. Do be careful on those rough paths and don't overtire yourself. Let the girls help you. Oh, dear—I'll go and put on the kettle."

She fussed about as Alice led the way onto the front verandah, which was almost closed in by dusty old creepers and rambling roses. There were piles of leaves banked in the corners and thick soggy cobwebs looping under the roof. The roses looked half dead, probably because two trees now loomed over the verandah, cutting out the sunlight. The wilderness seemed to be slowly covering the old house like a quilt. From the stone steps, a path went between the two trees towards a circular clump of tall shrubby plants and weeds about twenty meters away. There was more daylight down there.

Alice stood on the step and looked around. Violet had said that she hardly ever came out here now. "We used to sit on this verandah and wait for visitors to arrive," she said, almost to herself. "So many visitors. They would come up the drive there and around the fountain," she pointed to the shrubby clump.

"What fountain?" asked Sophie. "Did you really have one there?"

"Indeed—just a small one, but very elegant. Grandfather had it brought out from Italy. It's still there, but it doesn't work any more—not since it became rather overgrown."

"D'you mean it's under all that bushy stuff? Cool!" exclaimed Robbo. He and Ben raced along the path to peer through the dense, tangled thicket. They yelped as the shrubs scratched their arms and cheeks. Ben picked up a long stick and thrust it through the branches until it struck something hard. "Yeah, there's something in there but it's too thick to see much!" he shouted.

What must have been a circular drive around the fountain was now rather narrow, as bushes had grown across it and become tangled with weeds and the wiry trailers of creeping grasses. Alice hobbled to one side of the circle.

"Just through here, now—there should be a path somewhere," she murmured, feebly pushing at the bushes with her stick. "It goes down to the far side of the garden."

The boys sank down on their haunches, squinting under the bushes for signs of a path. "Wait a sec while we move this dead branch," said Robbo. He and Ben heaved aside a large fallen bough that was overgrown with creepers, and a way through opened up ahead.

"Yes, that's right." Alice went forward very slowly, while the boys cleared rubbish from the path. Sophie and I kept close to her in case she tripped, but neither of us felt brave enough to take the old dragon's arm. Occasionally she murmured to herself, "I had no idea that things had grown so much. It's so dark!"

As we pushed down towards the bottom of the garden, behind the Pyles' place, she stopped. "There, now—that's what I wanted you to see, those trees."

In the shadowy undergrowth it took me a while to make out what she meant, but gradually I focused on two massive trunks holding up a roof of branches that stretched halfway along the block and over into the street.

"Grandfather's oaks," said Alice. "He planted them himself when the house was built a century ago, one for himself and one for Grandmother. They grew beside the lawn and we would sit under them in the summer."

"Why did he plant oaks?" I asked her. "There must have been big gum trees here already. Wouldn't they have done?"

"Well, the new settlers didn't much fancy the gum trees—untidy, messy things!" I nudged Sophie—could anything be messier than what we were looking at! Alice went on, "Oaks last, you know, and they grow well in this southern climate. Besides, oaks reminded Grandfather of the Old Country."

"What Old Country?" Robbo mumbled.

Alice glared at him. "Why, England, of course. A hundred years ago most of the people living in Australia had come from the British Isles, or their parents had—it was still 'home' to them." She looked at Robbo more closely and then at Sophie. "You two, Roberto and Sophia, you ought to understand—don't your people come from Italy? Don't they talk about their Old Country?"

"Well, sort of. Dad's Uncle Leo is always going on about it, but he doesn't call it that," said Robbo. "Anyway, Sophie and I and Dad were all born here. We're Aussies."

"Hmm." Alice stared at the forest of baby oaks growing up under the two monsters. "I remember there was a farmer some miles away who came every autumn to collect the acorns for his pigs. Beedle would rake them off the lawn into five or six large heaps and the farmer would bring his horse and cart along here and load them up."

This baby oak forest must have once been the lawn!

"I didn't know pigs liked acorns," said Ben.

"Who was Beedle?" asked Robbo.

"Beedle was our gardener when we were children, but we've had others since then. The last one was Jackett—he was with us for well over thirty years."

"What happened to him?" asked Robbo.

"He was too old and couldn't manage the work. But he still comes to see us, and his wife, too. She sometimes helped in the house. They don't live far away."

It was quiet for a moment as everyone stared around. Mr. Pig Bottomley was right about one thing—the place was a jungle. I mean, a wild garden is great, much more interesting than our sort of tidy, clipped garden, but a wilderness needs a bit of organizing so that you can walk through it without busting your ankle or getting scratched to death or having an eye spiked out.

Then Ben asked, "Don't you have a gardener anymore?"—which was a pretty stupid question really when you looked at the chaos.

Alice turned away from the oaks and began to move back towards the house. "The young ones these days charge far more than we are able to pay, and they don't understand this sort of garden," she said in a huffy voice. "But now I'm tired. We'll go back inside and see if Violet has made the tea."

Sophie and I sighed. If only we could persuade Alice to go on talking!

We helped her back to her chair in the front room. She seemed exhausted and looked very old.

"I'd like to be left alone now," she said, leaning back in the chair with her hand on her chest. "You can tell my sister I'll have my tea in here."

"Thank you for showing us the oak trees," said Sophie, as she and I turned to go.

"Yes, I added. "No wonder you don't want a garage down there."

"There's no danger of that," snapped the old lady, "not while *I'm* alive."

Chapter 10

The boys were still outside exploring the fountain, so Sophie and I went along the passage to find Violet in the kitchen. On the way we snuck into the dark dining room for a quick look. There were eight heavy dining chairs with leather seats, four at the table and four more lined up along one wall. Against another wall stood a polished sideboard. The brown curtains were almost closed, and the room felt dead and stuffy, like a museum. But once there would have been a crowd in here every mealtime—Father and Mother Featherby, the four kids and maybe visitors, with a maid bringing in the soup or the roast beef, and the curtains pulled wide open to let in the sun, and flowers on the white cloth.

We both shivered a bit as we crept out. There were six or seven other doors along the passage, all closed. Sophie and I had to whisper.

"I wish we could look inside. I suppose these were the kids' bedrooms."

"And a bathroom—and they might have had a servant living here, too."

Alice and Violet probably used the two front bedrooms, one off the hall and the next one behind. The rooms seemed to get much smaller towards the back of the house, except for the big kitchen.

"Oh, you've come back again," exclaimed Violet, who was in there resting her foot on the stool. The kettles were fizzing on the stove, and the table was set out with cups. "Is Alice all right?"

"She's very tired and would like her tea in the front room. I'll take it to her," offered Sophie.

"Thank you, dear. I *knew* she'd overdo things. What did she want to show you in the garden?"

"The oak trees your grandfather planted—down there behind Pyles' place."

"Oh, of course—Grandfather's oaks." Violet began pouring the tea.

"I don't think Miss Alice could believe how everything had grown," I told her. "It was quite hard to find the path, and the acorns have all grown into little trees—it's like a forest down there."

"Oh dear. Jackett used to keep the paths cleared and the acorns raked up, but it's some years since he left and we never go down to that part of the garden now. The two big oaks are splendid, aren't they!"

"Well, yes—they're huge." Sophie took the little tray and carried Alice's tea to the other room.

I'd been trying to work out what Alice had meant about assets, so I said to Violet, "If you sold that piece of land to the Pyles, you'd be able to pay to have a new gardener or even a housekeeper."

"I suppose we would," sighed Violet, "but then those people, the Pyles, would cut down the trees for their car park, wouldn't they? There's no room for anything else with those oaks there."

"I know. That's why I'm confused. That piece of land

would be worth more if the trees weren't there, so why did Miss Alice call them assets?"

"Why?" Violet sipped her tea while she thought. "I suppose because they are beautiful, and big, and old, and wonderfully shady, and because Grandfather planted them for his family. Trees like that cannot be bought and sold—so perhaps 'asset' isn't the right word. They aren't like the cars and boats those people have next door." She gazed out of the window. "Just think—those trees were growing before cars were even invented."

I hadn't thought of that—it was pretty amazing. I tried to imagine the day when Grandfather Featherby had planted his oaks. If he was the snooty old boy in the portrait in the front room, he would have been dressed up in a high collar and a waistcoat, with his whiskers blowing in the breeze. Would he have just popped two fat acorns into the ground? Or maybe he gave orders to the gardener to plant seedlings. How could a gigantic tree like that come out of a nut, and keep on growing for a hundred years? I felt almost sick when I thought of a chainsaw slicing down a hundred years of such slow growing in just a few hours. I could hear the screaming saw as it sank its teeth into the great trunk, spewing out juicy white sawdust. Mum got upset enough when one dahlia was flattened by a soccer ball. "It's taken *months* to grow," she'd fume at Ben, "and you go and knock it over in a second without thinking." But what was a dahlia compared to an oak tree?

Sophie came back and reported that Alice was resting. "And she said again that she'll never sell that land while she's alive."

"Of course not," said Violet. "So much has been sold in our lifetime—this place has been almost swallowed up. It doesn't bear thinking about, what's gone—the stables, the orchard, the paddocks."

"Why did it have to be sold?" I knew it was rude to ask, but I wanted to know.

"Oh, to cover expenses," she sighed. "When Arthur died and when Father grew too old to run the place it all became too much. And the rates and taxes went up and up. The blocks where your houses are were the last to go, while our parents were still alive, but they hated parting with that land and the stables."

Sophie and I stared glumly at one another—I suppose we felt sort of guilty to be living there.

The back door slammed and the boys steamed in. "We've found a way in to the fountain!" announced Ben. "It really is there, but it's all full of junk."

"The middle bit is all streaky and there's a boy on top, blowing a sort of pipe," added Robbo.

"The fountain! I'd almost forgotten it!" exclaimed Violet. "We used to call that boy 'Arthur,' because he was like our little brother—or we thought he was. He blew water from his pipe up into the air and it sprinkled into the basin below. I expect Alice told you that Grandfather had it sent out from Italy—just the central part, which is made of bronze. He had the stone part at the bottom made here, and there were pink and cream waterlilies growing in it. The water sounded so cool and fresh on a hot day. Visitors coming in always stopped to admire it."

"I wish we could make it work," growled Robbo. "I bet my dad could fix it."

"Well, his name's Fontana—he ought to be able to," I said, rather smartly I thought.

Robbo's eyes opened. "Wow! That's right! I *bet* he's a fountain fixer. Can I ask him?" he pleaded with Violet.

"It would be so good to see it working again," she sighed, "but don't you think your father's too busy? And the whole garden bed would need to be cleared out so that we could see it. Oh, dear, I think we'd have to ask Alice, and I don't want to disturb her now."

Chapter 11

And just what have you lot been up to?" demanded Mum, who was in the back garden inspecting her dahlias when the four of us crawled through the hole in our fence from *Featherbys,* in the corner by the compost heap.

"Um…nothing much," said Ben, gazing at the grass.

"Only mucking around," added Robbo, looking sideways at us. It was amazing how those two could act so guilty. No wonder Mum was convinced we were heading for delinquency and ruin.

"Oh, it's okay, kids," I sighed. "I think we can tell Mum now—Miss Violet's foot is better, and that's what we weren't s'posed to talk about."

Mum stared. "Miss Violet's *foot?* Do you mean Miss Featherby?"

Sophie started to explain. "Well, yes. You see, she had a bit of a fall a few days ago, and…um, Jess and I happened to be there and we helped her inside and bandaged her foot and all that stuff."

"And we've been back a couple of times just to see if she needed any more help," I said. "The boys took in some firewood for her and even Vicky collected some kindling."

"Well…that was kind of you all, but why weren't you supposed to talk about it?" asked Mum.

"Let's go inside!" I began making peculiar signs towards the Pyles' place, where Sandra and Bartram were clattering round collecting bottles and plates after the party. They were back in their designer tracksuits. "We don't want the neighbors to hear!" I hissed.

When we were all seated around the kitchen table eating cake, Mum said, "Now, what is all this about and why all the secrecy?"

I took a big breath. "Well, we've discovered that the Featherbys have a horrible nephew called Mervyn Bottomley who's trying to get them out of the house so it can be sold."

"Yeah—old Bott," interrupted Ben. "He's rude and he slurps his tea."

"Shush, you," I said, not wanting to be interrupted now that I'd started this confession. "Anyway, *we* think the Featherbys didn't want anyone to know about the accident, especially Bott, in case Miss Violet was taken away to hospital, because Miss Alice wouldn't be able to look after herself and maybe they'd both get put in a home or something."

Mum clutched her head. "And what on earth have the Pyles got to do with it?" she asked. "Why didn't you want them to hear?"

Robbo butted in. "Well, you see, Ben and I and Jess were watching their stupid party through the fence, and suddenly old Bott turned up. Would you believe, he's a *friend* of theirs! We heard him telling Bartram that he ought to buy the Featherbys' land at the back of their place for a car park and a pool."

"And Bott didn't even let on that the Featherbys are his aunts," said Ben.

"Great heavens," said Mum. "Ben, see if you can find Dad. I'd like him to hear all this before it gets any more complicated."

Dad was in his den groaning over the accounts from his business. Dad's a printer. He likes printing but he hates accounts, so he was probably quite pleased to be interrupted and dragged to the kitchen.

"What's this all about?" he asked when he saw us sitting around the table. "Are you planning a bank holdup?" He winked at Robbo to show that it was a joke—Dad often makes feeble jokes.

"No way," said Mum. "We're not going to add any more offenses to the list! These kids have already been trespassing, spying, and eavesdropping."

"Oh, that's just great," groaned Dad. "What's been going on, then?"

"Tell Dad what you've told me," said Mum to us, "and try and do it one at a time."

When we'd finished, Dad seemed quite relieved. "Well, all I can say is that it's none of our business," he said. "The Featherbys will have to sort it out for themselves."

"Dad!" I wailed. "They're too old. And they don't want to leave—they've lived there all their lives."

"And you ought to see their grandfather's oaks—two of them, down behind the Pyles'. He planted them a hundred years ago and they're *huge*!" said Ben.

"I *can* see them, Ben," roared Dad. "The whole suburb can see them!"

"There's a fountain, too," said Robbo. "It's all blocked up and dirty but I'm going to ask my dad if he can fix it."

"Those poor old girls," sighed Mum. "It's very sad

when things get on top of old people like that. They should have moved out years ago and sold up. Still, the land must be worth a fortune now."

"No wonder the nephew has his eye on the place. Is he going to inherit it?" asked Dad.

"Well, we *think* so, worse luck." I frowned. "Bott will be the only one left in the family. It'd be all right if he was a nice person, but the Featherbys think he's just going to sell the place for the money and then everything will be bulldozed."

"Well, I'm afraid that's the way of it, and there's not much we can do about it," said Mum. "It might be just as well, really, as they've let it get into such a mess, and the house is almost beyond repair." She glanced at her watch and jumped up. "Ye gods, I must go and collect Vicky from the party this minute."

Through the window we could see Bartram and Sandra moving the Volvo and the Mercedes from the street back into their drive. Their back garden was spotlessly tidy again after the party and all hosed down. What a pain!

"Huh," snorted Ben as Mum headed for the car and Dad returned to his accounts. "*They* weren't much help. I thought they'd have some ideas."

"Mm. Hopeless," I agreed with Ben, for once. "Parents are always desperately busy doing something else when you need them."

"Well, let's go and tell *my* dad about the fountain," said Robbo, "just to see if he knows how to fix it. Come on...if we all go, he might take more notice."

Mr. Fontana had a visitor, his old Uncle Leo. Since the accident, Uncle Leo often came around to see if he could cheer things up, but Uncle Leo was a widower, too, and the pair of them often ended up feeling more sorry for themselves than before. They were looking pretty dismal now.

"Hi, Uncle Leo," Robbo greeted him, and before the men had a chance even to say hello, Robbo raced on, "Do you two know anything about fountains? There are lots of fountains in Italy, aren't there?"

"Sure—I guess so," agreed his father.

"Ah! The best in the world—big ones, little ones, all so beautiful!" enthused Uncle Leo, cheering up at once. "Near our town, where I grew up, there was a villa—so large! And with such gardens, *magnifica*! You should have seen the fountains and cascades—waterfalls and jets. All bubbling—ah, *molto belle*!" His eyes were closed as he remembered.

"But d'you know how they *work*?" demanded Robbo. "Someone in our family must have known once, if we're called Fontana, mustn't they?"

Joe Fontana shrugged. "Maybe there was someone, but it would have been a long time ago. Just because we're called Fontana…it doesn't mean anything. You know, like all the people called Smith—almost none of them would know how to be a blacksmith or to shoe a horse, would they!"

I'd never thought about names having meanings like that. "Gee, I wonder what Huggins means?" I grinned. "Our ancestors probably invented bear hugs."

"How about Bottomley?" sniggered Ben.

"Oh, shut up," groaned Robbo. "We're not talking about horses or hugging or bottoms; it's fountains we want to know about."

"Why?" sighed Mr. Fontana. "There aren't any around here."

"There's one next door, see!" crowed Robbo. "The Featherbys have got one and it came from Italy, but it's all blocked up and it doesn't work. Would you be able to fix it? *Dad*?" Robbo stood there like a fast bowler appealing to the umpire.

The men stared at him. Of course they didn't believe him, you could tell.

"How do you know about it?" asked Mr. Fontana, suspiciously.

"The old ladies told us, and we've seen it. But it's all hidden behind bushes and weeds, and it's full of junk and dirt. There's a boy on top with a pipe and the water squirts out of that, Miss Violet said, when it works."

"Have you kids been sneaking around next door and bothering those old ladies, while my back's turned?" Joe probably thought Ben and I were a terribly bad influence.

"It's *okay*, Dad—the Featherbys don't mind, and we've been helping them a bit, but the place is in an awful mess."

"You don't have to tell me," grunted Mr. Fontana, probably thinking of the fence pickets he had never got around to fixing. "Well, I don't know much about fountains, but I suppose I could have a look at it over the weekend to try and find out how it works."

"You're a good boy, Joe," beamed Uncle Leo. "I'll come, too, for a look. I might remember something. It's probably just dirty and blocked."

"What do the old ladies say? Have you boys asked them, or is this just your crazy idea, eh? They mightn't want anyone messing around with their fountain." Mr. Fontana wasn't making it easy, but of course parents never do.

"Miss Violet would like it to be fixed, I know," replied Ben, "but she says we have to ask Miss Alice. She's the old bossy one."

"Well, just you do that. I'm not setting foot in that place until the bossy one has given me the go-ahead."

"We'll ask her tomorrow morning!"

Chapter 12

*N*ext day the boys began rushing into *Featherbys* as soon as breakfast was over.

"Hang on!" I yelled as I saw them heading for the hole in the fence. "It's only 8:30, idiots—Miss Alice won't be up yet. She takes ages to get going, and you don't want to make her more snitchy than usual, for heaven's sake!"

Ben and Robbo hung around the yard doing their bowling ballet while the time dragged on. When they made another attempt at 9:30, Mum dragged them back, but by 10:30 they could wait no longer. Mum insisted that I go in with them to make sure it was all right.

We found Violet at the kitchen table looking at a couple of old books.

"Oh, I'm glad you've come," she greeted us. "I want to show you something." The books were albums of faded photographs, and Violet turned the pages until she found what she wanted. "Here it is—a snapshot of the fountain in the old days, do you see?"

We all peered at it—yes, the boys could recognize the figure on top blowing his pipe, but everything else looked quite different. There were no shrubs or creepers around the fountain hiding it from view, just a circular bed full of flowers. Two children stood on a narrow path that ran around between the stone basin and the flowerbeds, and on the drive beyond stood a pony and carriage with a man and a woman sitting in it.

"Cool," exclaimed Robbo. "It's so tidy!"

"Who are the two kids?" asked Ben.

"They are Joyce and Arthur, our sister and brother. They were just a bit younger than you then, I think. And that is Father driving the carriage with Mother beside him under her parasol. Father bought a car soon after that, but he always liked using the carriage for short journeys around Bottlebrush, in good weather."

Father Featherby sat up straight in a high collar and tie and a stiff-looking suit and hat. He was holding the reins and a whip and staring into the distance. You couldn't see Mother Featherby's face at all, as the parasol threw a dark shadow all over her top half. She must have been really spooked about the UV rays.

"Look, there's the path down to the oaks, the one that is all grown over now—there on the other side of the fountain," Robbo pointed, "and you can see the oaks at the back. They weren't half so big then, were they—nothing was! You could see the sky and the garden was all sunny."

"Well, this picture was taken over sixty years ago, so the trees have had all that time to grow since," said Violet. "I wish Grandfather could see them now."

"Where are you and Miss Alice? Why aren't you in the photo?"

"I think Alice must have been taking it. She was given a camera when she was about seventeen and we had great fun with it. I was probably helping her and telling the others to keep still. Quite a lot of the photos in this book were taken by us. Look, here's another one of the fountain from closer."

"Yeah, see, Ben, the boy's blowing his pipe upwards," said Robbo, "and the water falls down into that little basin just below him and then it overflows from that into the big basin at the bottom."

"And there are the waterlilies I told you about," Violet pointed "Beedle would lift them out in their boxes every winter and tidy them up. Oh, now here's a photo of Alice and me when we were grown-up—out on the verandah steps."

The boys jostled to have a look, and I craned over their heads, but I couldn't recognize the two smiling young ladies in their rather shapeless outfits and pointy shoes. Their hair was short and almost hidden under peculiar flowerpot hats. The verandah posts were covered in flowering roses.

"Is that really you?" gawked Ben. "Gee."

Luckily he didn't have a chance to say any more because Robbo suddenly remembered what they had come for. "Dad says he'll try to fix the fountain but we've got to get permission first. And Uncle Leo could come, too, because he can remember lots of fountains in Italy and he might be able to help. Do you think Miss Alice would let them come this afternoon?"

"Goodness, so soon!" gasped Violet. "I haven't said anything to Alice yet because she's been rather tired and upset. She's still in bed, I'm afraid." The boys looked so disappointed that she went on, "Well, just a minute, I'll go and see what she says. It's very good of your father and uncle to offer to mend the fountain, but I think that Alice will worry about the cost."

"But it mightn't cost anything!" exclaimed Robbo. "Dad thinks it's probably just dirty and blocked, and he doesn't want any money just for cleaning it."

"Really? How very kind of him—people hardly ever do things for nothing these days, I find. Well, in that case, I'll go and ask Alice what she thinks." Then she picked up the photo album. "And maybe I'll take this with me."

Violet still used her stick, but she was no longer limping. When she returned, she looked rather sad.

"What's the matter? Did she say no?" Robbo asked, anxiously.

"Oh, not at all—she said yes, and she said your father is very kind to offer. It's just…I don't know…she seems to have lost interest in everything, ever since yesterday. I think it upset her to see what has happened to the garden. She hardly ever goes out there now, you know, and I don't suppose she realized how quickly a garden can get out of control. She just doesn't know what to do about it—and neither do I. Oh dear, if only Mervyn were different!" By then Violet was talking to herself.

"Did she look at the photos?" asked Ben.

"Ah, yes—she can remember taking them in springtime. She even remembered that the flowers around the fountain were pink and white, although the colors don't show in these old photos. She said she always loved those beds around the fountain."

"I bet she'd like them to look like they were then," decided Ben. "We could give her a surprise."

"It would be very hard work," frowned Violet, looking at the two fairly small boys in front of her. "But, I've just thought of something. Jackett and Mrs. Jackett are coming to see us this afternoon. You remember, he was our last gardener, and they visit us from time to time. Perhaps if your father came while they were here, he could ask Jackett about the fountain—I'm sure it worked in his day—and you could ask him what to do about the flowerbeds."

"Wow! Let's go and tell Dad!" Robbo and Ben rushed off.

"Come later on, when we've had our tea," Violet called after them. She smiled at me. "Jackett always did like his cup of Indian tea."

Chapter 13

Our fountain-fixing squad lined up on the Featherbys' front verandah late in the afternoon. There were seven of us waiting when Violet opened the door—five kids, Joe Fontana, and Uncle Leo.

"Goodness, look at you all!" exclaimed the old lady. I noticed that her hair was tidier, her stockings were straight, and she wasn't using the walking stick, although she still wore my bandage under the stocking.

Sophie introduced her father and Uncle Leo to Miss Violet, who said, "It is very kind of you both to bother about our poor old fountain! The boys will show you where to go and I'll bring Jackett out. He has to take things slowly with his arthritis—perhaps you could carry out a chair for him to sit on, Ben. I don't think he can stand for long. And my sister won't come out just now—she'll be tired after the visitors."

Robbo led us all down to the clump, while Ben brought a chair from the kitchen. We were soon joined by Violet and the Jacketts.

The Jacketts were not quite as ancient as the Featherbys, but old Mr. Jackett was bent and stiff, I suppose after all those years of digging and slaving in the garden, and, like Miss Alice, he hobbled along with a stick. Apart from the stick and the hobbling, there was nothing else on our Geriatric List that really applied to the

Jacketts. Mrs. Jackett was large and full of talk. She had a big, beamy sort of face and she wore bright blue.

"Just fancy you children wanting to fix the old fountain!" she exclaimed. "It would do my heart good to see that thing sprinkling again."

"No worries! We'll try to make it sprinkle for you!" beamed Uncle Leo. "It will be beautiful again, you'll see!"

"Well, I dunno," grunted Sophie's dad, who was in his usual gloomy state. "How are we going to get at it through all these bushes and prickles?"

"It's all rubbish, that," announced Jackett, who had settled down in the chair with his stick across his lap. "It needs cleaning out. Now listen, there are stone paths through the bed to the fountain...you know, like spokes in a wheel." He pointed with his stick towards the round bed. "Should be a way in there, and another over there and the third around the other side. And then a path all around the basin in the middle."

"I've brought out the old photograph," said Violet. "Here, you can all see how it was, with the little paths in through the flowers."

Everyone crowded around to check.

"Is it okay then if I prune back some of these bushes?" Mr. Fontana asked Violet.

"Oh, I think so, if Jackett says they are rubbish," she replied.

"Yes, rubbish I said. Don't just prune 'em—dig 'em out. Get rid of the rotten things!" You could tell that old Mr. Jackett was enjoying himself, giving orders and watching others doing the hard work for a change.

Joe Fontana had brought his tools, and gradually he cleared a way through with a hand saw and a spade, cutting away branches, digging out roots and clumps of weeds. Uncle Leo helped us to drag everything away into a pile and to tug at trailing creepers. Slowly the side of the fountain showed up and Violet cried, "There he is—little 'Arthur' up on his pedestal!"

"Yes, there he is!" echoed Mrs. Jackett. "He seems to be in one piece, bless 'im, but isn't he dirty and all covered in bird mess!"

Joe had cleared the first path through and was now uncovering the stone paving around the fountain by scraping off layers of dirt and weeds with his sharp spade. As he made space, we all squeezed in to peer over the side into the basin.

"Pooh!" squawked Vicky. "It's yukky!"

The bowl was clogged up with weeds, dead branches, rotting leaves, some rusty cans, and at the bottom a thick layer of black slime. The stone was stained and crusty with shriveled moss, and there was a fairly awful smell.

"There's something pretty dead in there—probably a rat or two," sniffed Joe. "It'll all have to be scoured out. We'll need a wheelbarrow."

"There's an old one in the woodshed," shouted Ben, running off.

"No wonder it won't work," grinned Jackett, hoisting himself up to have a look into the fountain. "That's a muckheap and no mistake." He settled back comfortably to watch. "It began to go bad not long before I left," he recalled. "You remember that big drought about ten years back?"

"No," said Vicky, staring at him. "I wasn't born."

"You weren't born? Great snakes, I don't suppose you were!" wheezed Jackett. "Anyway, we weren't allowed to use the fountain then or to fill it, and it pretty well dried up—just a few inches of sludge left in the bottom, and the lilies all died, too. And by then I was too stiff to do much about it."

Ben bumped his way back with a rickety wooden wheelbarrow and an old shovel he had found in the shed, and the two boys jumped into the fountain and began scooping out the mess. They seemed to enjoy the perfume of dead rat. Luckily there were only two shovels and not much space, so Sophie and I led Mrs. Jackett down the jungle path to see the oaks, with Vicky trailing after us. The air was much fresher down there.

Mrs. Jackett gasped at the forest of tiny oaks in the gloom beneath the two giants. "Well! To think that used to be the finest lawn for miles around! What a real shame to see it let go."

"The Featherbys can't afford a gardener now," I said. "Miss Alice says the young ones are too expensive." I felt as if I had to apologize for the old ladies who had let the garden go to ruin after all Jackett's years of work.

"I daresay," agreed Mrs. Jackett. "You know, there were two full-time gardeners here when Mr. Jackett started. Not long after the war, it was, but things were beginning to go wrong at *Featherbys* even then. The other chap retired and Mr. Jackett then had to do all the work. I came to help inside sometimes when the old Featherbys were still alive, but Miss Violet had taken over the running of the house during the war, when the servants left."

"How many servants did they have?"

"Why did they leave?"

Sophie and I were both bursting with questions. Mrs.

Jackett was the sort of person Mr. Scrooby would call a Resource.

She gazed up into the branches. "Let's see—there would have been a cook and a housemaid and the gardeners, and they probably had someone in to help with the laundry as well. Anyway, when the war came people weren't supposed to have servants—they were all needed in the army and to make munitions and to help on the farms and the like. I had a job in a grocer's shop when I left school!"

"Why didn't Miss Alice and Miss Violet get jobs?" asked Sophie. "You know, instead of having to sell off the land."

"Listen to you!" exclaimed Mrs. Jackett. "In those days, ladies like them didn't go out to work, and anyway what could they have done? They weren't really trained for anything, were they! They were stuck here looking after the house and the old folks. Things would have been different if Arthur had come back, I daresay."

"Why would they?"

"Well, they all expected him to take over this place and bring up a family here. It's a place that needs young folks with energy. It would have been left to Arthur, him being the only son."

"Why? Do you mean just because he was a man! That's *typical*—what about the three girls?"

"Well, that's mostly the way it was done in those days. The property went to the son who carried on the family name, while the girls were expected to marry and their husbands would provide for them. Anyway, the Featherbys never got over it when Arthur was killed. Everything just went to pieces. And then there was all that trouble with Miss Joyce, too."

"Do you mean when she died?" asked Sophie. We were both nervous about interrupting too much in case Mrs. Jackett clammed up, but she wasn't really the clamming sort.

"Oh, not just when she died, no, although that must have been dreadful of course, someone of her age with the cancer—and that husband of hers refusing all offers of help from the Featherbys. I heard that he'd hardly even let them see her when she was so ill. But no, the trouble I meant was earlier—when she married him. Almost eloped they did. Mind you, Miss Joyce was always a bit flighty, they say. She liked a good time. Spoiled, probably. Got in with some funny people, and her parents didn't like that Gerald Bottomley one bit. Not their type at all. They thought he was fast and unreliable and nowhere near good enough for a Featherby, and they tried to stop her marrying him, but she was over twenty-one and off they went. And the war was just starting—folks do silly things in wartime, getting themselves hitched up to people they hardly know, in all the excitement."

Sophie nudged me and nearly caused a giggling attack because Mrs. Jackett talked in this funny way like one of those windbags in a TV soap. Luckily she didn't notice the nudge—she just went rolling on with the story.

"Well, next thing, Gerald Bottomley had joined the Air Force and was off overseas for years, leaving Joyce behind here, at *Featherbys*, with the baby. I suppose the little grandson Mervyn was a bit of a comfort to the old Featherbys after Arthur died, even though the child wasn't a real Featherby to them. Anyway, after the war Gerald Bottomley came back and the feud began all over again, and he and Joyce weren't a bit happy together either. They moved into a little flat somewhere. When she got ill and died, Gerald grabbed young Mervyn and moved to another state. Said he didn't want the boy falling back into the clutches of that high and mighty Featherby lot."

"But he's come back now," I said. "Mervyn, I mean."

"My word, he has—his father's dead now. I suppose he discovered that this property hadn't been sold and that he would be the only one of the family left after these two old aunts, and he was back quick smart, snooping around." Mrs. Jackett seemed to be very sniffy about the Bottomleys.

"Is he married?" asked Sophie.

"No, he never did marry. He's by himself. No children."

"Who ever would want to marry Bott!" I spluttered.

"It's a pity he's not nicer," sighed Sophie. "The Featherbys could do with someone to look after them, and it sounds as if he's probably lonely, too. It's all a stupid muddle. They don't seem to be able to talk to one another."

"Well," sniffed Mrs. Jackett again, "his father set young Mervyn against the Featherbys because of what had happened in the past. The boy's mind was poisoned. And I suppose he can hardly remember his mother."

"Really?" Sophie looked surprised. "I don't think I'll ever forget *my* mother. I hope I won't."

Mrs. Jackett patted Sophie's shoulder. "Of course you won't, dearie—but then you were just a bit older than Mervyn was, when...it happened, and anyway you've got a nice loving family who'll always keep her in mind."

Vicky was bored by all this talk and was finding little tracks through the baby oaks. When she had pushed through as far as the first enormous tree trunk, she suddenly called out, "I've found an old seat!" She climbed onto it and waved to us across the little forest.

"That'll be right,"' said Mrs. Jackett. "There was two of them—one under each tree. Nice old stone benches to sit on and admire the view." She frowned at the jungle that was hemming us in. "Huh, view indeed! The benches'd be nearly as old as the fountain, I'd say."

Sophie and I were already wading through to reach Vicky on her seat.

"Let's try and clear some space around it," I said. I grabbed a small oak sapling and heaved. After some struggle it suddenly came out, waving its long skinny taproot with the old acorn husk attached. I almost fell over.

"That wasn't too hard," I puffed. "Come on!"

"This leaf mold stuff is still nice and loose." Mrs. Jackett was stirring it with her foot. "The roots will come away easy—but you wouldn't want them to get much bigger. Once those oak roots get down into the real earth, they'll grab on like the very devil."

"Quick, then!" cried Vicky, scrambling down from her seat and seizing a tiny stalk. "Don't let them grow any more!"

The three of us tugged and heaved, with Sophie and me tackling the bigger plants and Vicky cleaning out the small ones underneath until we'd cleared a fair space around the old stone seat. We sat on it in a row, grinning.

"Look at you!" laughed Mrs. Jackett. She pushed towards us and examined the seat. "It's not too bad, is it— not cracked or broken. Just needs a good scrape and scrub, I'd say, especially that fancy carved bit around the edge. Ooh, they don't make seats like this any more!"

"I'll scrape and scrub it, because I found it!" Vicky decided. "You two can clear away more trees." Vicky was getting as bossy as Miss Alice.

"Thanks very much, you!" I said. "But first we'd better see how they are getting on with the fountain. That'll need scraping and scrubbing, too."

Chapter 14

Next morning the Fontanas' new washing machine nearly went into orbit. When Ben and Robbo had finished scooping out the big basin, they'd looked like victims of an oil slick disaster, and the dead rat perfume had come home with them, more smelly than ever. Mr. Fontana was all grimy and sweaty, too, after grubbing all the old shrubs and weeds out of the round bed.

Sophie told me to bring Ben's filthy clothes in, and we did the whole lot together on the heavy soil cycle. We poured some lavender-scented disinfectant into the rinse water to clear the air a bit.

"You wouldn't believe that the Featherbys once had servants, would you," I said to Sophie, as we waited for the spin-dry cycle to finish. "Imagine all that land and stables and an orchard, and two gardeners and someone to do the laundry, and a cook and a housemaid! It's weird how things can go wrong in families."

I had a sudden twinge, remembering Mrs. Fontana, but Sophie didn't seem to notice my tactless remark. I'd been thinking about families a lot since we'd met the Featherbys, and how each one was different and why. What would have happened to the Featherbys if Arthur had come home and if Gerald Bottomley had been killed instead? What would happen if Mr. Fontana married again? Or supposing Mum had been hit by the car instead of Mrs. Fontana? Or what if the Pyles had an unplanned baby instead of an asset? Families could change so quickly. The Featherby family had almost died out, just in one generation—unless Bott hurried up and produced a kid or two!

Sophie must have been thinking of *Gone With the Wind,* which we'd seen on video, because she suddenly said, "The Featherbys are a bit like the O'Haras—remember Scarlett and her sisters, and their gorgeous dresses and the parties they had?"

"Wow, yes!…and then the American Civil War came and there was almost nothing left. Mrs. O'Hara died and Mr. O'Hara went mad and they all nearly starved. Remember that bit when Scarlett had to eat raw turnips out of the field? Yuk—raw turnip must be disgusting!"

"Well, the Featherbys aren't quite *that* desperate," giggled Sophie. "Imagine Alice munching a turnip! But it was a war that sort of messed things up for them, too. Oh yes, and that reminds me—last night Uncle Leo told us that his older brother was in the Italian army in Arthur's war. That was our Great Uncle Carlo. He was in North Africa, too, and he was taken prisoner. But guess what—the Italians were on the other side!"

"You mean they were fighting against the Australians? In Africa? But why? That's crazy—and here *we* are living next door to each other and being friends! Why do people have stupid wars?"

If Mr. Scrooby had heard us, he would have told us to research the Second World War. He was always boring on about Research. Perhaps we would do the war as part of our school history syllabus sometime. It might be just a bit more interesting now that I knew about Arthur and

Gerald and Great Uncle Carlo. What on earth was Arthur doing in the North African desert? Where did Gerald Bott spend all those years flying around with the Air Force? And why was Uncle Carlo an "enemy"? It seemed an awfully long time ago.

The spin-dry clicked off at that moment and brought us back to the 1990s.

Later in the morning our squad (minus Sophie's dad and Uncle Leo) arrived at *Featherbys* carrying buckets, scrapers, brushes, and rags. I was also armed with a garden fork and a rake for an attack on the oak saplings.

We called at the back door to tell Violet that we were going to clean the fountain and the stone seat.

"You don't tell me!" she said. "And even Vicky has come to help!"

"I found the seat all by myself," explained Vicky, "and I'm going to scrub it."

Violet's eyes were bright. "I've decided not to say much to Alice about what you are all doing. She won't notice from inside the house, so we'll wait and surprise her when it's done, I think." I suppose Violet didn't really expect us to finish the job, so she wasn't going to raise Alice's hopes.

"Dad's going to try and unblock the pipes in the fountain when we've cleaned it all up," Robbo told her. "He'll come in after work one day."

When we arrived at the round bed I said, "Why don't we all clean the fountain first and then we can all go and grub out the oaks while Vick scrubs her seat."

"But I want to do the seat *now*!" complained Vicky.

We all glared at her until Sophie had an idea. "Look,

Vicky would be the best person to clean the boy on top of the fountain because she's the only one of us who's small enough to stand in the little bowl up there."

"Aw, but I want to clean him," whined Robbo.

"And so do I," whined Ben. Kids are an acute pain. But when it came to bribery, Sophie was the tops—she'll make a great mother.

"Okay then—if you boys want to clean all the rest of the fountain by yourselves, too, then Jess and Vick and I will go and do the seat and the oaks. We'd rather do them anyway—they're much easier." Sophie picked up the fork.

The boys looked at the dirty stone basin, which had an outside as well as an inside, and all the grooves and twiddles on the bronze parts of the fountain. It was a killer.

"Oh, all right then," muttered Ben. "I s'pose Vicky can do the statue if she wants to. I bet she won't do it very well."

"Okay, Vick?" I asked.

"Yes, I'll scrub the little boy if you'll help me up," agreed Vicky, "but I'm still going to do the seat by myself later on."

The scrubbing and scraping was awful. We grazed our knuckles on the stonework and bumped heads and elbows on bronze corners, and our arms and backs ached as we tipped slimy water onto the garden and lugged buckets of clean water from the tap. Tempers boiled over as our hands and knees stung and bled and we collided with one another and scratched ourselves on the spiky shrubs and breathed in lungfuls of dead-rat smell.

"There'll be another load of stinking washing tomorrow," sighed Sophie.

"Stop tipping slime in my hair!" I shouted at Ben.

"I never thought it would take *this* long," groaned Robbo.

"He's nearly clean!" squeaked Vicky, hanging onto the fountain with one hand and wiping little "Arthur" with the other.

The rest of us stood up clutching our backs, and looked. "Arthur" stood gleaming greeny-bronze against the sky, playing his pipe.

"Wow, Vick, that's great!"

"You've got rid of all the bird poo and cobwebs!"

"Wait till Miss Violet sees him—I bet she'll cry!"

Vicky stood ankle deep in dirty water, smiling at "Arthur." You could tell she'd fallen in love with him.

"I'll just scrub all the bottom bits," she called down, "and then we can scoop all this mucky water out of the little basin."

It was amazing how we suddenly perked up again once we'd seen "Arthur" shining in the sun. Like mad things we scraped the flaky old moss and dried mud off the stone and scrubbed at the dirty black watermarks. Now and then someone would hose down the parts we had done to wash off the loosened grime. Bit by bit the old fountain brightened up—like Violet, who was looking more jaunty every day since we'd met her.

Vicky began swooshing the dirty water from her small basin. Then all five of us bucketed out the big basin and, after a final hose-down, it was done! We stood back and stared.

"It's funny, but I can't remember what it looked like before we started," I said, doubtfully, "I suppose it really is cleaner?"

"Well, we'd never get it to look like new—after all it is

a hundred years old, isn't it. It's supposed to look old," said Sophie firmly, "and anyway it smells better."

"Here comes Miss Violet," whispered Vicky. "Let's see if she notices."

Violet toddled down the overgrown path towards us, on her fieldmouse legs. When she reached the clearing, she stopped and exclaimed, "Oh, 'Arthur'—you dear boy!" Then she walked right around the fountain. "And look at the stonework—it's all bright again! And the bronze too—it's that proper sort of bronzy green. Oh it *does* look beautiful! Thank you all so much—you must be worn out!"

We all collapsed in a heap on the ground. We *were* worn out and hot and filthy and bleeding, but very pleased with ourselves.

"Now, I've made a big jug of orange cordial and some sandwiches, if you'd like to come into the kitchen," said Violet Featherby. She must have sent to the grocer for an order. I bet she hadn't had so many people to lunch for years, especially people stinking of dead rat.

Chapter 15

This vacation was the short spring one, so we had less than two weeks left to finish what we had started at *Featherbys*. Once our parents had decided that we weren't actually vandalizing the place or terrorizing the old ladies, they were quite pleased that we'd found something "sensible" to do. If we were busy scrubbing seats and mending a fountain we were less likely to be roaming about the streets looking for trouble. That's what they were thinking in their usual muddled way.

We weren't doing these things at *Featherbys* because they were *sensible*. They weren't very sensible at all, and probably that's why we were enjoying ourselves. Sophie and I could hardly believe that we'd found a way of keeping the kids occupied without wrecking Mum's garden or turning on the TV at 9:00 A.M. Vicky, for once, was able to do things that the rest of us were doing, which made her feel grown-up. The boys waded into the action jobs as if they were at a school camp, and I reckoned their interest would just about hold out until the end of the holidays, as long as they had regular time off for demon bowling.

Sophie was a different person since that day when we'd crawled through the fence. Somehow Miss Violet seemed to be filling the gap in Sophie's life—not that she was a bit like Sophie's mum, but she could have been a grandma or a great-aunt. They had a lot in common, really, Sophie and Violet. Both of them had to battle to keep their households going, and one of them was too old for the job and the other one too young.

I went into *Featherbys* as if I was climbing back into another age. It was like adding pieces to a jigsaw picture each day as I found out more about the Featherby family and the old days in Bottlebrush. I suppose Mr. Scrooby had been right, really—interesting things do happen, even in your own boring old suburb, and I had found them right next door without needing to change my name to Dalrymple or de Quincey!

We spent a whole day hauling out the baby oaks from under Grandfather's two trees, while Vicky scrubbed the old seats. Our hands were nearly wrecked, but the big oaks looked like proper trees again after we'd carted away all the weeds and saplings and raked the earth clean and level around their great furrowed trunks. The new oak leaves overhead were a bright cheerful green.

Uncle Leo and Jackett surprised us when they turned up one afternoon. They had already become good mates. Jackett shuffled around the garden showing us things that were half buried or quite hidden under the weeds and creepers—patches of bulbs struggling through the grass, a sundial almost strangled by a vine, and a little statue of a girl imprisoned in a bush. There were old roses and lilacs and flowering apples that all needed rescuing from grass and creepers. He looked quite pleased when he saw the oaks and the ground under them all raked clear.

I didn't know much about plants, except for Mum's dahlias. Up until then, *Featherbys* was just a sort of muddle of bushes and creepers and flowers to me, but when Jackett told us their proper names each plant became real and separate, like a person. My favorite names were *love-in-a-mist* and *honeysuckle.*

As he showed us the shrubs, Jackett said, "All you can do now is untangle 'em, and tidy 'em up a bit, then prune them hard next year ready for the spring."

"*Next year!*" cried Sophie. "But our vacation ends next week!"

"Gardening's a slow old business, young lady," chuckled Jackett. "There's a right time for things to be done, by the season, and you've missed it this year! It learns you to be patient." He looked around the jungle. "At any rate, it would take an army of real gardeners to put this place right again, not just a flock of kids."

Jackett might as well have slapped us in the face! After all our *slaving!* We just stood there feeling hopeless. I suppose the worst thing was that deep down I knew Jackett was right.

Uncle Leo did his best to cheer us up. "Hey, *someone* has to start it, and look what you kids have done in just a few days. It's good, really good! Tell you what, we'll get that fountain working pronto, eh! Then I help you with the garden bed—we'll get those flowers in quick and then we weed the big path around the outside. One thing at a time, eh? Roma, she wasn't built in a day!"

Sophie gave him a small smile. The rest of us just stood there.

"Oh, well, that soil needs fixin' up if you want to grow flowers there," sniffed Jackett, pointing to the bed around the fountain. "You can cart in some of the oak-leaf mulch from under the old trees—that's grand stuff—and I've got a bag of chicken manure for you in Leo's trunk."

"Okay!" beamed Uncle Leo. "Looks like you got your army of gardeners already. Oh—and Joe is coming in after work to fix the fountain. If she works okay, then tomorrow we fill her up and whoosh!"

"The fountain isn't a she," said Vicky crossly to Uncle Leo. "Its name is 'Arthur'!"

Mr. Fontana arrived as promised after work, clanking in with lots of tools and pieces of pipe. He and Uncle Leo climbed into the fountain, where they poked and prodded, screwed and unscrewed, shouted, turned the hose on and off, and fiddled about for what seemed like hours, getting very wet and dirty. We all hovered around and sometimes one of us was told to hang onto something or to turn the tap on or to get out of the way. Violet fluttered in and out of the house so often that it was a wonder Alice wasn't suspicious.

"Now try," shouted Uncle Leo for the twentieth time. Robbo turned on the tap, and after a short silence there was a gurgling sound, then a splutter, and finally a watery explosion as a stream of black muck shot out from the end of "Arthur's" little pipe all over Mr. Fontana and Uncle Leo. Everyone yelled! Gradually the spray turned from black to gray and then to clear water, sparkling in the evening light and making the bronze fountain shine green as the mist floated down.

"That's got it!" laughed Joe Fontana. "Doesn't it look beaut!" He hadn't beamed like that for a long time.

Violet could hardly speak. She was probably weepy, but it was a bit hard to see in the dim light. Sophie and I did a hug and dance routine, and the boys climbed into the basin to get sprinkled on. Vicky just stood there gazing at "Arthur," the little green boy that she had scrubbed clean.

"Okay, turn it off!" called Uncle Leo. "Tomorrow we clean out all this muddy water and hose everything down, then we fill her up with the fresh water and she's ready to go!"

"Not *she*—HE!" shouted Vicky.

Chapter 16

We slaved away for the rest of the week, filling the fountain with clean water, heaving out roots, and tipping loads of leaf mold and manure into the round bed. Uncle Leo helped us to dig it as we weren't much good with the spade. We also tried to clear the circular driveway of weeds and straggling shrubs as best we could, and finally we planted the round bed with seedlings that Jackett brought along in lots of little boxes he called "punnets." He said the plants were pink and white ranunculus. Vicky called them "nunkles."

Sophie said we should have a special turning-on ceremony to give Alice her surprise, and we chose Saturday so that Mr. Fontana could be there, too. Mum and Dad actually asked if they could come as well.

Violet said that if we arrived at about eleven, Alice would be up and dressed. We all marched in through the front gate instead of the hole in the fence, and we really made quite a big crowd in a circle around the fountain—five Hugginses, four Fontanas (with Uncle Leo), and Mr. and Mrs. Jackett. Joe Fontana tested the fountain once or twice, so that we wouldn't have an embarrassing failure, then Sophie and I went to the front door and rang the old bell.

Violet answered it, all twittery, and called Alice to come—she was wanted in the garden. Alice of course was in a grump and not very keen to hobble outside, but in the end she came, thumping her stick crossly. "What *is* it?" she kept snapping, as we led her down the path.

Vicky was in charge of turning on the tap, and just as the two old Featherbys reached the edge of the driveway, "Arthur" began to squirt water through his pipe as the fountain burst into life again. We all clapped and it felt like some important opening ceremony. We'd even brought some folding chairs for the old ones to sit on. I was sorry the Mayor of Bottlebrush wasn't there in his robes and chain, but I suppose Dad was good enough, being Councillor Huggins.

Violet was weepy and laughing and quite dithery, but it was hard to tell what Alice thought. She just sat on her chair staring at the fountain and softly tapping her stick on the gravel. Mrs. Jackett began chattering and said there really ought to be a speech on such a lovely occasion, and Jackett announced that the seedlings we'd put in were looking pretty perky, really. Mum raved on about the trees, and Dad examined the sundial that we'd unstrangled and tried to read the time from it, but we five were all looking sideways at Alice.

Suddenly she raised her stick and we all shushed.

"Mrs. Jackett is quite right," she said. "There should be a speech and I shall make it. You people have made me and my sister very happy today. You have brought the fountain back to life and we are most grateful for that, but it is even better to see the garden full of friends after being empty for so long."

Sophie nudged me—Alice had called us friends and there were actually tears in her eyes—dragon's tears! Mum snuffled into her handkerchief for a minute, but not for long. We started clapping again and Dad took some photos. I couldn't wait to compare them with the ones in the Featherbys' album.

Alice again began remembering the old days when their visitors came along the drive from the front gate, pausing to admire the fountain and the waterlilies.

"That's what we've forgot!" roared Jackett. "Those blessed lilies! But I know where to get some and I'll bring 'em next week."

As he spoke, I heard the gate creak. A man was ducking his way past the privet hedge. We all turned to see Mervyn Bottomley walking towards us.

Sophie softly groaned, "Oh *no!*" and I heard Ben's loud whisper to Mum and Dad, "It's Bott! You know—the one we told you about, their nephew."

Bott eyed us suspiciously as he approached. "What's all this then?" he asked, trying to sound hearty.

Alice took charge with one of her starchy speeches. "Good morning, Mervyn. It is rather propitious that you should arrive now, just as the fountain has been restored to life."

"Oh yeah?" grunted Bott, looking at it. "Queer old thing, isn't it—I don't think I remember it." But he sounded rather uncertain. He would have been about five when he left *Featherbys* after the war—as old as Vicky. I bet *she'll* never forget the fountain as long as she lives!

Alice said to him, "Hmm, I'm surprised you don't remember it—even though you've been away so long. Your great-grandfather put it there in the early days. The statue reminded us of your Uncle Arthur when he was a child, so Violet and I think of it as a sort of memorial to him."

"It's called 'Arthur,'" Vicky told him, rather crossly. She could look like a thundercloud if she tried.

"Is it just—well, I don't remember *him* either. Before my time, *he* was."

The sniffy way Bott talked about his Uncle Arthur, whom he hadn't even known, seemed queer to me, almost as if he was jealous. Probably Alice kept reminding him that Arthur should have inherited *Featherbys* and that it was an awful tragedy that he'd died in the war. All that wonderful uncle stuff wouldn't improve Bott's temper one bit.

He sniffed at the fountain. "Well, if you ask me, it's a waste of effort doing the thing up."

"Why ever do you say that, Mervyn?" quavered Violet.

"Well it couldn't be in a worse place, could it!"

"It's in exactly the *right* place, Mr. Bottomley, if you don't mind my saying so," interrupted Mum, to my amazement. "It's in the center of things, where everyone can see it—or they will be able to when a bit more clearing has been done."

"That's okay *now,* maybe," shrugged Bott, "but it's in a hopeless place for subdivision. It would be the first thing to go." He eyed the fountain more closely. "Mind you, that center bit—bronze, is it? Could be worth a bit if you knew the right dealer."

That "center bit" included "Arthur's" statue, of course! I felt like screaming or turning the hose on Bott full squirt. He'd ruined everything, the pig of a man.

Mrs. Jackett was spluttering, "Well! I *ask* you…" while Violet clutched a handkerchief to her face. Alice sat there as cold as stone, almost like a statue herself.

"Thank you for your opinion, Mervyn," she said. "Now I think you'd better go."

"Right! There's gratitude for you—I merely came to see how you both were, but I know when I'm not wanted. *Goodbye.*" He turned and stomped off. From the gate he called back, "Don't waste your time on this useless jungle—a bulldozer's the only way to go!"

Chapter 17

Sophie and I were sunk in misery after that. The turning-on party had fizzled out, and we all trailed home lugging the folding chairs, while Violet helped Alice inside and shut the door. They thanked us again for all our trouble, but we could see how upset they were and wanting to be alone—alone to think about "Arthur" being bulldozed or carted away to a dealer.

Sophie and I sat on our back lawn gloomily chewing grass stalks.

"I can't believe that one person could wreck everything like that," I fumed. "He's *horrible.* Just when we were getting on so well and even sour old Alice was sweetening up."

Sophie flung herself flat on the grass. "I know. But now I don't feel like doing another thing in there. What's the point, with Bott talking about bulldozers."

One amazing thing came out of the morning's fiasco, however, as we found out at lunch—Mum and Dad were all fired up! Mum announced that Mr. Bottomley was an Unspeakable Man. "The nerve of him...spoiling everything and being so tactless! He obviously hasn't much family feeling."

"He must be very sure of inheriting *Featherbys* to behave like that," said Dad. "Do we know if the place is held in trust for him?"

"What's that mean?" asked Ben.

"Well, it means going back to his grandparents' wills, probably—that's the old ladies' parents. They could have left the property to Alice and Violet to use for their lifetime, and in trust for the grandson Mervyn after Alice and Violet die. That means that the old ladies can live in it or let it, but they couldn't sell it or leave it to anyone else in their wills. It would have to go to Mervyn Bottomley when they die. From the way he's behaving, he must be expecting that to happen, otherwise he'd be more careful about upsetting his aunts. If it's *not* held in trust for him, they could change their minds—and their wills—and he'd miss out."

"That's just what he deserves," I grunted.

"But what about the Pyles?" Ben suddenly spluttered through a mouthful of cheese roll. He chewed madly and did a big swallow. "Remember? We heard Bott telling Bartram to make the old ladies an offer for some of their land. That sounds as if they *can* sell it."

"Jove—that's right, Ben!" Dad slapped the table and an apple rolled off the fruit bowl. "In that case, he's being overconfident, I reckon."

"Yes—he's sure that *Featherbys* will go to him because he's the only one of the family left, and the old ladies are just crazy about their family," I said. "Family's more important to them than anything, even if it's only Bott."

"He must be getting really impatient, waiting for them to die," said Mum. "He's not getting any younger himself, and greedy people are always in a hurry. But I must say he's taking a risk talking about bulldozers and subdividing, the way he did this morning. If *I* were his aunt I'd change my will on the spot. It would be a crying shame to lose that old garden, just for the sake of more boring brick veneers. There are so many treasures in there that ought to be saved—like those oaks."

"But *you* always said the trees were a menace," said Ben. "Make up your mind, Mum!"

"Well, I suppose I just hadn't thought about it properly," admitted Mum. "That Bottomley fellow has made me think about it, and I reckon you kids are doing the right thing, trying to save it." At least Mum was honest.

Dad was gazing at the wall. "I wonder if the old ladies could do with some advice?" he muttered. "Or if they'd like someone just to talk to?"

"Dad! You were the one who said it was none of our business!" I reminded him.

"Yes, Harry—you can't interfere, not unless they actually *ask* for some help, and I can't see Miss Alice Featherby doing that—she's very proud," said Mum.

"No, I suppose not," he sighed. "We mustn't rush them, but you kids can keep an eye on things and let us know if there are any sinister developments! You've still got another week off school, and I guess you have plenty more jobs lined up in there, eh?"

Vicky had been wriggling like a worm on a hook during all this legal talk, but she brightened up now. "Yes, I'm going to scrub the statue of the girl. Miss Violet says I can call her 'Victoria'."

"After Queen Victoria?" asked Mum, as if Vicky would know who *she* was.

"No—after me," said Victoria Huggins.

Chapter 18

After lunch I went to tell Sophie that Mum and Dad had seen the light about *Featherbys* and that I felt just slightly more hopeful. Sophie was feeling better, too, because her dad and Uncle Leo had been so wild about Bottomley that they'd drunk a whole bottle of Chianti between them during lunch and had ended up shouting things like "La Vendetta!" before they fell asleep in the armchairs. And Mrs. Jackett had called to say that she would drop everything and come at a moment's notice if she was needed to lie down in front of a bulldozer.

"I wonder how the poor Featherbys are feeling?" I sighed. "They haven't got anyone to talk to about it." We found ourselves drifting towards the hole in the fence.

"We'd better not disturb them, I guess," said Sophie, "but there's no reason why we can't go on weeding or untangling vines. If Violet sees us and *wants* to talk she can come out."

We moved quietly through the jungle towards the front of the house. All our comings and goings were opening tracks through the undergrowth, as we trampled down the weeds and pushed rubbish aside.

As we came near the fountain I heard a man's voice. "Listen!" I warned Sophie. "That's not Pig Bottomley again, is it?"

We slid under a thick curtain of creeper and peered through the leaves. A man and a woman were coming up the drive from the gate, picking their way rather fussily past the rubbish we'd heaped up.

"It's the Pyles—Bartram and Sandra!" Sophie hissed.

"What do *they* want? Don't tell me they've come to make an offer for the land—what a day to choose!"

Sandra was just as glamorous as she'd been for the alfresco lunch party, except that her outfit featured a calf-length straight skirt with a slit and a pin-striped jacket and a floppy velvet cap thing, and her accessories were brown and gold to match.

"I hope she doesn't knock poor Violet over with one of those earrings!" I whispered. Sophie and I had to clamp our mouths shut with our hands so as not to snort.

Bartram had on a navy jacket and bow tie over gray slacks—so he looked a lot better than he had in the bush hat and drunken ostrich getup.

I wished we could leap out from behind our creeper and chase them down the drive with rakes, yelling like enraged savages. It was awful that the old ladies would have to face the Pyles so soon after the shouting match with Bott—they were upset enough as it was. I had to keep reminding myself what Mum and Dad had said, that it was none of our business. These were grown-up things to do with money and property. Who would take notice of kids like us, even if it was our business?

At least we had warned Alice and Violet about the Pyles, so the old ladies were sort of prepared. Sophie and I crept up behind a bush, closer to the house.

Bartram and Sandra mounted the stone steps and

ducked under the groping creepers and onto the verandah. Bartram smoothed his very smooth hair with one hand, then pressed the old doorbell. Sandra peered in a horrified way at the cobwebs overhead and shuddered, then arranged herself in a charming pose and stuck a smile on her face. I could hear them clearing their throats as they waited.

Bartram was about to push the bell again, when the door opened just a little and we could see Violet's wispy white head. Bartram had his speech all ready.

"Good afternoon, Miss Featherby. It is so good to meet you. We are your new neighbors down at the far end, at the back. This is my wife, Sandra, and I am Bartram—Bartram Pyle."

Before Violet had a chance to breathe, Sandra swooped. "Delighted to meet you, Miss Featherby, and I am looking forward to meeting your sister, too. My goodness, what a very old house this must be, and such a large garden! However do you manage?"

Sophie and I were making vomit faces at one another. Violet said something that we couldn't hear, and she certainly wasn't opening the door any wider or asking them in.

Bartram began again. "Oh, dear, I am distressed to hear she is not well. How unfortunate. We certainly won't impose on you if that is the case. Perhaps you would both read this instead, when your sister is feeling more herself." He handed over a long white envelope. "I took the precaution of bringing it with me in case you were not in."

Violet took the envelope and seemed to be saying goodbye and trying to close the door.

"Goodbye for now, Miss Featherby!" crooned Sandra, dipping towards Violet with the golden earrings swinging. Sophie grabbed my wrist as we smothered our snorts. "I do hope your sister will recover quickly. It must be a worry for you when you have so much else on your mind." Her glance swept around the whole jungle and the unswept verandah and the rusty downspouts.

"Goodbye!" beamed Bartram. "We'll expect to hear from you soon. You'll find all our business phone numbers listed on the letterhead in there, as well as the home number and the car phones. You can contact one of us at *any* time or leave a message on any one of the answering machines. Goodbye for now!"

Violet hurriedly closed the door as the Pyles went down the steps. She'd got rid of them pretty smartly. I wondered if she knew what an answering machine was, and I bet she'd never heard of a car phone.

"How do you think that went?" muttered Sandra as they passed our bush.

Bartram shrugged. "Hard to say. Damned nuisance we didn't see the other old girl—Merv says she's the boss lady. Still, when they read our proposal and think about it, they'll probably jump at the offer. It looks as if they could do with some extra funds." He gazed around. "What an appalling bloody mess!"

They tried to push their way down to the oaks and "their" bit of land, but gave up when Sandra snagged her outfit on a rosebush and Bartram ran smack into a spider's web.

"Oh hell, it's ruined!" screeched Sandra, unhooking her skirt, while Bartram clawed cobwebs out of his sleek hair and made spitting noises. Sophie and I nearly died laughing behind our bush.

The Pyles hobbled through the weeds down to the gate, stopping every few paces to stare and poke at things, and finally they vanished. We heard two car doors bang and an engine start up and purr smoothly away around the corner.

Sophie and I stared at each other. "They *drove* round! Just half a block—in the Mercedes!"

We collapsed into the grass, waved our legs in the air, and laughed ourselves silly again. It was good to feel all limp, like spaghetti.

While we'd been fixing the fountain, Violet had been in and out all the time to see how we were getting on, but we hardly saw her during the next couple of days. She seemed to be holed up in the house. We didn't expect to see Alice—she always stayed inside anyway.

At first Sophie and I wondered whether Violet was sick, but then we noticed her slipping out of the back door for something and she looked all right, and there was smoke coming from the kitchen chimney.

"Blow it all!" said Sophie. "Let's knock and see if they're okay."

Instead of calling us to come in, as she usually did, Violet opened the back door and stood there. She looked tired and gray-faced.

"Oh it's you, girls."

"We just wanted to see if you are all right, and whether you need anything," stammered Sophie. "Firewood...or milk, or anything...."

"Thank you, dear...no, I think we have everything we need. Alice and I have a lot on our minds just now, so

I won't ask you in. Oh, by the way, Mr. and Mrs. Pyle called—I was glad that you'd warned us about them, as it could have been a rather upsetting visit otherwise."

Sophie and I weren't going to let on that we'd seen it all from behind a bush, and Violet didn't offer to tell us any more, so the white envelope remained a mystery.

"Well," I said, "if you need us we're down in the garden a lot of the time."

"I'm surprised that you want to go on with that, after what Mervyn said," sighed Violet.

"We were a bit put off at first," said Sophie, "but we've decided that it would be silly to give up now."

Nobody mentioned bulldozers, but I bet we were all thinking about them.

While we sat clawing weeds and grass away from a patch of bulbs, Sophie and I tried to sort things out. We only had to listen to our parents to know that the land at *Featherbys* was worth heaps, and I suppose blocks of land are worth a lot more when they are stuck together. I mean, you could build a row of shops or office towers or a supermarket, instead of ordinary houses. That thought made us groan—even the Pyles' four-car garage and pool and wilting palm trees sounded better to live next to than a supermarket.

If Alice and Violet sold *Featherbys*, they'd have to find another place to live, but Bott was always discovering units for them and the old ladies would be rich enough after selling *Featherbys* to buy a really good unit, so that didn't seem to be a problem. Except that old people don't like moving.

But now that Bott was talking about bulldozers, and now that the Pyles had made an offer, which would mean cutting down Grandfather Featherby's oaks, what would Alice and Violet decide to do? No wonder Violet looked upset.

"There's something else," frowned Sophie. "Supposing they cut Bott out of their will, who will they leave everything to instead? He's the only one left in the family."

"Gosh, I don't know. They'd probably give it to some charity—but then the charity would probably sell it anyway to get the money. Oh, heck!" I moaned, yanking out a thistle. "I just wish we *knew*—it'll be awful if we're slaving ourselves to death like this for nothing!"

Chapter 19

We went back to *Featherbys* on Monday because Jackett was bringing the waterlilies, and Vicky wanted to scrub the dirty little statue she called "Victoria."

Jackett came in Uncle Leo's car because the waterlilies were in plastic tubs filled with wet earth and they were heavy. We couldn't see any lilies—just a knobby lump in the middle of each tub that Jackett said would soon sprout lily leaves and then flowers.

Ben and Robbo offered to lift the lily tubs into the fountain—it was a good excuse to get sopping wet. Once the tubs were sitting on the bottom we couldn't do anything more except wait for them to grow. Jackett told us that one lily was pink and the other cream, just like the ones in the old days.

Uncle Leo had brought a cart hooked on to his trailer hitch. "I think this path will look nicer if we move all the rubbish," he said, pointing at the piles of weeds and junk from the fountain and the oak saplings and dead branches we'd hacked down. "You kids help me load it on and I'll take it to the council depot to be mulched, okay?"

Vicky was busy talking away to "Victoria" and sloshing her with soapy water. She and the statue were about the same size. The rest of us started dragging and wheelbarrowing the mountain of rubbish down through the gate and out into the trailer. On about our fifth trudge we met an old man coming in. *Featherbys* was getting overcrowded—people always seemed to be ducking through the gate these days! This old man was wearing a dark suit and a hat, which he raised to Sophie and me as he went past. Under the hat he had nice silver hair.

"Good morning, young ladies!" he said.

"Good morning," we mumbled back, trying not to giggle. We weren't used to gentlemen raising their hats to us like that.

As he reached the fountain he slowed down. "My word!" he remarked. "It is most gratifying to see that in action again. Most gratifying!" and on he went up to the front steps and rang the bell.

That word "gratifying" sounded just right when he used it, like Alice's "grievous loss." He seemed very pleased that the fountain was squirting again, as if he remembered it from earlier days. We could see him raising his hat to Violet as she ushered him into the house, although we tried not to stare.

"I wonder who *he* is?" I said. "The Featherbys are having hordes of visitors lately, aren't they."

Jackett lowered himself stiffly onto the rim of the fountain. "I'll tell you who he is—he's old Plumpton. He used to be their lawyer, way back." He jerked his thumb towards the house.

"Their lawyer!" Sophie and I chorused. Could this be a hopeful sign?

"Mind you," Jackett went on, he doesn't practice the law now. He's retired and his son is head of the firm these days with some partners. *Plumpton, Headstone, and Silk* they are now." Jackett was watching us with his sharp old eyes and I bet he knew what we were thinking. "Old

Plumpton has known the Featherbys for many a long year—more like a friend really. He'd be the chap they'd turn to for advice, I reckon."

I told Dad and Mum all this while we were eating dinner. Dad now asked for a nightly bulletin, and I felt like a private investigator reporting on the Featherby Case.

Dad agreed that Mr. Plumpton's visit might mean that the Featherbys were thinking about their wills. "Even if it was just a social call, you can be pretty sure that the subject of Bottomley would come up—the old ladies must be thinking of nothing much else at the moment," he said.

"Mr. Plumpton noticed the fountain," I told them. "He said it was very gratifying to see it working again."

Sure enough, Mum smothered a grin as I used that word, because it sounded silly coming from me, but all she said was, "That's good—he's another one who wouldn't like to see it bulldozed."

"Sophie and I are wondering what the Featherbys will do if they don't leave the place to Bott," I said. "There's nobody else left in the family to leave it to."

"Yes, that is a problem, especially for someone like Alice Featherby, who sets such store by the family line," said Dad.

"Is Bott what you call a black sheep?" Ben asked. "I've heard of families having one—is that what he is?"

Mum laughed. "I suppose you could call him a black sheep—he certainly doesn't match the rest of the flock, or the two that we know."

"That's because he takes after his Bottomley father and not his Featherby mother," grinned Dad.

"Well, Mrs. Jackett told us his mother was a bit flighty,

and pretty well eloped with Gerald Bottomley," I informed them. "Maybe she was a black sheep, too!"

"What's eloped?" asked Vicky.

"Come on," said Mum, stacking up plates, "It's time to clear the table, I think!"

"Eloped means she ran away," explained Ben, who likes questions to be answered. "She ran away from *Featherbys* with Bott's father."

"If *I* lived there I wouldn't run away," Vicky announced, "because my friends 'Arthur' and 'Victoria' live there, too, and they need me to look after them."

Chapter 20

The next night Mum made another gourmet meal. She doesn't often get carried away in midweek, so it was probably because it was our vacation and we were being left alone a lot that she was driven to it by guilt. Trying to give us what those eggheads on TV call "quality time." We'd been into *Featherbys* during the day, messing about, but none of us had felt like working much and there was still no sign of Violet, so I guess Mum was trying to cheer us up. She certainly livened up the house with smells of bacon and onions and her own pizza sauce.

We'd just about finished feasting when Ben's nose began twitching, "Urk—what's that smell?"

"Onions and pizza sauce, you nut!" I groaned. "The whole house reeks of it."

"Not that smell—there's a new one." He went to the window and then to the back door. "It's smoke," he called. "Pooh."

"Someone must be burning rubbish," said Mum. "It's probably the Pyles—no one else would choose this time of night!" She began to clear the dishes away. "How about reporting them to the Council!"

I peered out of the back door, but it was too dark now to see much. The screen of Featherby trees loomed black against the sky, but there was a smell of smoke all right.

Dad answered the phone as it rang. "Hi there, Joe...it's Joe next door," he relayed to us. Then, "What! Are you sure? Okay...yes, right away...yes, yes, okay, give us a minute." He banged down the receiver. "Joe says there seems to be a fire at *Featherbys*—he can't really see what's happening through the trees, but from his place he can see a glow, and there sure is a smell of smoke now." We were all sniffing.

"What about Violet and Alice?" I yelled.

"Joe and I are going in. Now, listen—I don't want any arguments." Dad took charge before we all exploded out of the house in a panic. "Mum—you stay here with Vicky, and ring the fire department at once...then the ambulance. Jess and Ben, if you promise to do *exactly* as I say, you can come with me because you know the way around in there. Put on wool sweaters over your jeans, and heavy shoes and socks, while I grab a flashlight and some blankets...and be quick!" No one argued.

Mum was on the phone to the fire department as we ran next door. The three Fontanas were already heading towards the fence and the smoke was thickening. Joe had another flashlight and some tools.

"Right, kids—show us the quickest way through all this tangle, but *don't* run ahead. Stay together."

Sophie took her dad's flashlight and we led the way to the path and through to the back of the house, where the smoke was swirling across the yard. Already we were coughing and rubbing our eyes.

"It's that chimney up there," Dad shouted. "It's on fire!"

"That's the kitchen chimney, the one over the big

stove!" Ben told him. Flames were flaring and roaring from the top.

"Do you think Violet is in there—in the kitchen?" cried Sophie. "She might be trapped!"

"Well, the light isn't on," gasped Dad. "Stand back and I'll look through the window. Is that it?"

"Yes, the one on the verandah, and that's the back door—see if it's open!" I yelled.

"Have they got gas?" Joe Fontana was flashing his flashlight about.

"Yes—in the kitchen!"

"The meter's over here, near the verandah," Dad called between coughs, and Joe yanked a wrench out of his pocket and rushed over to shut off the gas. I suppose you think of things like that when you are a builder.

Dad was battering on the back door, which was locked of course. Violet had told us that Alice had extra big bolts put on all the doors. Dad shone his flashlight through the window, then he lurched back to us, coughing hard. "Can't see anything—the blind's down, but it's very smoky. This back part will go up like matchwood if the fire gets into the roof. Is there a hose?"

"Only the one around by the fountain," Robbo gasped.

"That'll take too long—we'll have to wait for the fire department. Quick, girls, where are the Featherbys likely to be? Will they be in bed yet?"

"I don't know!" I wailed. "Alice might be. Come around the front...oh, hurry!"

Flames and sparks began to swirl up higher from the chimney and through cracks in its sides. "Listen to the draft roaring—it's like a north wind!" yelled Joe Fontana. "They must have left the flue open on the stove and I bet the chimney's caked with soot!"

"Look!" Dad pointed towards the roof. "There's smoke coming from under there—come on!"

As we ran, I remembered how the stove had blazed and roared when the flue was open. Poor Violet—had she forgotten to shut it down? She'd been so worried lately that she probably wasn't thinking straight.

We bashed our way through the tangled garden and around to the front steps. My heart flipped over—there was a light in the front room! Dad started banging on the front door and ringing the bell furiously, making a frightful din.

"Miss Featherby! Are you there! Open the door!" he bellowed.

"Don't frighten them, Dad, they'll think it's a break-in! It's *us*, Miss Violet—it's Jess and Sophie!" I yelled. "Quick! You *must* open the door—your kitchen is on fire! Oh, *please* hurry!"

I jumped up and down while Sophie went on knocking. After a couple of minutes that seemed like hours we heard Violet's voice behind the door. "Is that really you, girls?"

"Yes, yes…it's *us*, Sophie and Jess! You must be quick!" Slowly the door opened a crack and Violet peered at us like a terrified bird. "Whatever do you want?"

Smoke was creeping down the passage behind her and swirling about the hatstand in the hall, like a ghostly octopus. Violet hadn't even noticed it.

"There's a fire in the kitchen! Where is Miss Alice?

You *must* get out of the house at once! Quick—unchain the door—oh, hurry!"

Eventually she did and Dad pushed the door further open and eased his way past Violet, who was quite bewildered. "A fire? What do you mean? I lit the stove as usual—is that what you mean?"

"It's okay—she's in here!" we heard Dad shout from the front room.

I squeezed past and ran in. Alice was sitting in her usual chair. One hand was clutching her chest as she stared in fright at Dad.

"It's all right, Miss Alice—it's me, Jess, and this is my dad—you know him. There is a fire and you aren't safe in here! Please—you must get up, come on!" I tried not to shout, but I felt like screaming at her.

Alice didn't move. Her face was horribly white and damp and she was breathing in a noisy way with her mouth gaping. Dad strode to the door and called, "Here, Joe, quick!" Mr. Fontana arrived and without speaking he and Dad picked Alice up between them and carried her outside. Sophie had already wrapped a blanket around Violet's shoulders and was trying to get her down the steps, but Violet struggled feebly and kept gasping, "Alice...where's Alice!"

I don't know what made me do it, but I turned back into the room. On the floor beside a chair was an old handbag, which I grabbed. I knew it was Violet's because she had paid us money for the milk out of it. Then I scooped up an armful of the photographs in their silver frames and heaved them into an old wood basket that sat on the floor by the hearth. I grabbed the two albums, which were on the table, and piled them on top. Through the haze of smoke Grandpa Featherby stared down at me from the wall.

"You'd better come too," I gasped at him. There wasn't time to climb up, so I grabbed the frame on each side and yanked. The hook flew out of the wall, and I shoved the picture into the basket. Luckily it wasn't too huge, like some family portraits.

"JESS!" yelled Dad. "Come ON—the roof's alight!"

Thank goodness I could now hear sirens howling and whooping in the street, and I heard Joe Fontana shouting at Robbo to take the flashlight to the front gate and show the ambulance men the way in. Ben rushed in looking for me, so I pointed to the basket and together we lugged it outside.

"What on earth's all this stuff?" he yelled at me, between coughs.

"Shut up and just carry it!" I shouted back as we staggered down to the fountain, coughing our heads off. Sophie was down there still clinging to Violet and several flashlight beams were lurching towards us down the drive as Robbo guided the ambulance men in. Thank goodness Uncle Leo had cleared away the rubbish!

Someone called, "The firefighters are going in from the back, where the fire is!"

In all the confusion and darkness I saw stretchers. Dad and Mr. Fontana were helping to lower Alice onto one, tucking a blanket over her, and the ambulance man said to Sophie, "Is that another old lady? We'd better take her along, too. Another stretcher over here!" he shouted. It was all so quick. In no time, Alice and Violet were being carried down to the gate and the ambulance was wailing on its way.

Only then did I turn around and look at the house—its roof was blazing! A wall of flames rose high from the back part, with columns of sparks spiraling above. Thick smoke was now funnelling through the front doorway, where we'd been minutes before! There were terrifying noises—spitting, cracking, thumps, exploding glass, shouts, but mainly the eerie roar of the fire.

The six of us stood gaping, feeling the blaze scorch our faces. Even Ben was too overawed to say more than "Wow!" I vaguely wondered if we should be trying to save anything else.

Then Dad snapped us out of it. "Come on—there's no point staying here. Mum will think we've all be incinerated. We'd better go out the street way."

"Will the garden burn?" I asked him.

"I don't think so—the firefighters will have the fire under control fairly soon, and things are pretty damp out here anyway. Lucky there are no gum trees to explode."

Sophie helped me lug the basket. "Clever you to save these!" she said, when she realized what was in it.

"Now all stay together," shouted Dad. "Don't you boys run on ahead!"

The street alongside *Featherbys* was in chaos, blocked by two fire engines and with hoses coiling and writhing over the ground like giant pythons. Passing cars had pulled up anywhere they could, and groups of people stood staring, their faces colored orange by the flames and the red flashing lights on the fire trucks. It could have been a weird disco, almost.

Several policemen were trying to sort out the muddle and to keep onlookers back. The firemen had hacked a slice out of the hedge to give them an easy way in, and now they were jetting water onto the blazing roof. The rafters stuck out like burning ribs. "Keep back!" yelled a fireman, as a slab of roof collapsed in a storm of sparks.

"Gee!" cried Robbo. "Look! The kitchen's all gone!"

It was hard to make out what was happening, but he was right. The old chimney stood smoking and steaming, but in front of it, where the main part of the kitchen had been, where we used to sit around the table with Violet, where the passage, the pantry, the back verandah had been—had all fallen into a smoking heap of rubble. Dad had been right—the back part had gone up like kindling. There were flames coming through the front roof now and the old woodshed was smouldering, too.

I saw that Sophie was crying, and my own sore eyes were stinging with tears and the beastly smoke. "Let's go home," I croaked to Dad, and we struggled on with our basket load, over the snaking hoses and through the sheets of water to our own street.

Mum and Vicky were in the Fontanas' backyard, trying to see through the trees. "Thank heavens you're all right!" shrieked Mum. "Are you all here? What about the old ladies? We've been terrified for them!"

"They're okay—we got them out in time, thanks mostly to the girls," said Dad. "The ambulance has taken them to the hospital."

"Why?" asked Vicky, whose eyes were huge.

"Just to make sure there's nothing wrong, Vicky—you know, they probably breathed in a lot of smoke."

Later I heard him tell Mum quietly that Alice was worse than that, and it looked to him like a heart attack.

"In any case, we'll have to get hold of Bottomley," sighed Mum. "He *is* their next of kin, after all. Oh heavens, what a terrible night!"

Chapter 21

It is very hard to sleep when the house next door has just burned down. I lay in bed with stinging eyes and a scratchy throat, and everything around me seemed to stink of smoke. We'd all had showers and I'd washed my hair, but the stench still clung on. Mum had helped us to bathe our eyes and to put drops in them, and she'd piled all our smoky clothes into the laundry and shut the door. The fire was out, but a couple of firemen were patrolling the ruins in case it sparked up again. Dad told me he'd spoken to one of the policemen about the basket of things Sophie and I had carted away from *Featherbys* for safe-keeping, so that we wouldn't be arrested as looters! I lay there thinking that I could have spent the night in jail, just for doing someone a good turn!

I was pretty sure Sophie wouldn't be asleep either. She'd be thinking of Violet and Alice in their hospital beds, surrounded by strange people and objects and wondering whatever had happened. I wondered if Alice was very ill. Mum had rung the hospital during the evening, but they hadn't told her much except to ring again in the morning.

Dad had tracked down Bott in the phone book and told him the news. At first, Dad said, Bott had been angry. "I've known all along that something like this would happen!" he'd shouted, as if it was all Dad's fault. "Those stupid old fools, thinking they could go on living there in that deathtrap—and only last week I told them I'd found a unit close by that would suit them perfectly." Bott said he'd come around in the morning. If his aunts were safely in the hospital, there wasn't anything more he could do at that hour of night. He didn't thank Dad for saving their lives or anything.

There wasn't anything more any of us could do, except think...and cough...and rub our eyes...and toss about...and go on thinking. It was crazy that the old house had gone, just like that. I must have gone to sleep in the end because I woke up when it was next morning and I could remember dreaming of Alice's white, clammy face and its gaping mouth. The stink was still in my nostrils when I woke, but my eyes felt a bit better.

Mum had already rung the hospital. Violet was "resting comfortably" she was told, but Alice's condition was still "critical." They wouldn't tell Mum any more because she wasn't a relative, so she gave them Bott's name and phone number, in case he hadn't bothered to tell the hospital himself. Mum wasn't going to let him get away with anything.

I dressed quickly and went to find Sophie. Her eyes were bloodshot and she hadn't slept well either. I knew she wouldn't. "We'd better go and look," she said. She meant look at *Featherbys,* of course.

We crept through the back way and went as close as we could without being seen. We didn't want to be told by some bossy fireman or police officer to keep away. The smell was sickly in there—it made our noses curl. Under the trees there was a sprinkling of burnt leaves, although only the branches close to the house had been scorched.

The front brick walls and chimneys of the house were still standing, but we couldn't get close enough to see what had happened inside. Windows were broken and the old bricks were smeary black, and most of the roof was burnt with black charred rafters sticking out against the sky. At the back, as we'd seen the night before, there was just a crazy heap of mess. The kitchen chimney pointed up like a crooked finger and at the bottom we could see the stove. The oven doors were twisted on their hinges, but still there.

"Look," whispered Sophie, "the kettle's on top." It was, too—lying on its side, ashy-gray and buckled—the kettle we'd filled to make tea.

"I wonder how many cups of tea it made in all that time?" I said, blearily. You think of stupid things.

There was no sign of the table or the dresser or the chairs—just a mess of coals and white ashes with piles of twisted roofing iron higgledy-piggledy on top. Violet's old metal bucket had rolled out to one side and was half buried in ash. We couldn't tell what else was buried in there. Now and then there would be a tiny explosion in the ashes and a puff of sparks. A fireman was walking about, so we didn't go any closer.

It was still very early. Sophie and I went home to our place. Robbo and his dad were there, too, and Mum was fixing a neighborly breakfast, which seemed to be needed. She hadn't asked the Pyles to come but we could see them through the window, rushing about hosing the ashes off their assets and looking rather cross.

We told the others what we'd seen next door, and of course Ben and Robbo wanted to dash in at once to look for themselves. Joe Fontana roared at them. "Sit down and eat your breakfast, you two! It's still dangerous in there, and you are to keep away until the fire is quite out and the building has been made safe."

"Aw—the girls went in! It's not fair...." grumbled Robbo.

"Well, they shouldn't have," said Mum, "but at least they had enough sense not to go too close. I can just imagine you boys running straight into the hot ashes without thinking—and probably wearing sandals."

"The front walls of the house are still there," I said. "What about all the things inside? Will there be anything left to be rescued?"

"Is that Bottomley fellow coming around to see to all that?" Joe asked Dad. "I could board up the doors and windows if that's what he wants."

"Huh! Who knows what he wants, apart from the land," snorted Dad, spreading honey very thickly. Dad had announced that honey would soothe our smoky throats, so the jar was three-quarters empty already.

"Bottomley won't care about the house," predicted Mum. "In fact, I bet he'll be quite pleased about the fire."

"Pleased!" Sophie stared.

"Yes, pleased. Look, he's been trying to move his aunts out of the house for ages, hasn't he, and now they've gone and they won't be able to come back to that ruin. And second thing, the old house is probably not worth saving now, so the block of land it's sitting on will just have to be cleared—and that's exactly what he wants."

"And Alice is nearly dead in the hospital," I groaned, "and I don't suppose poor Violet will know what to do." I could almost feel the bulldozers rumbling down the street.

"I think I'll stop by the hospital on my way to work this morning," Mum decided. "At least I can leave Violet's handbag for her, and if she would like it perhaps you two girls could visit her this afternoon after I get home. She'll need someone, if Alice is so ill, and I can't imagine that Bottomley would cheer her up a lot—if he even bothers to go. In fact, I would nominate him as the world's worst hospital visitor."

"And I'd second that," munched Dad, scraping out the last glob of honey.

Ben had left the table and was at the window watching Sandra hosing down the boat. Suddenly he said, "Uh huh—Bott isn't visiting the hospital now—he's visiting the Pyles!"

"Really?" Mum had a peep. "Don't let them see us snooping," she snapped, as the rest of us scrambled out of our chairs. "Keep well back."

Bott was talking hard to Sandra and Bartram, who kept on hosing. Bartram was now squirting the cement drive and wasting huge amounts of water.

"Huh!" said Mum, as Bott walked briskly down to the gate. "I *told* you! They'll be sharpening up the chainsaw, if we're not careful, to start clear-felling the oaks."

"Hold on, dear, things haven't got to that stage yet," said Dad. "I think we still have a few tricks up our sleeves."

What tricks? we all wanted to know, but we didn't find out because the doorbell rang. Everyone froze and several of us said, "That'll be BOTT!" It was, too. Thank goodness Mum and Dad were still at home to deal with him. I was glad, too, that the Featherby photos and Grandpa's portrait were stored away out of sight—I don't suppose Bott would have wanted them, but I bet he would have taken the silver frames and sold them to some low-down dealer.

Bott had a lot to say. He'd already checked out the wreckage next door. "The house is a write-off, I'd reckon," he pronounced, "and the water has ruined a lot of the stuff that wasn't burnt. Most of it was rubbish anyway. There are a few bits of furniture the firemen dragged out, and I'll arrange to put them into safekeeping."

In your own place, I bet, I thought.

Mum was glaring at him rather meanly. "Have you given any thought to Miss Violet—after she comes out of hospital, I mean—where she is to go?"

"Well, I can't have her in my flat, if that's what you're getting at," snapped Bott. "I can't look after her and I have no space. If we could free up some of their money, I could see about the unit I've had my eye on for them. It's probably still on the market. In the meantime she'll have to go to an old people's home or something."

"I see," said Dad. "By freeing up money, I suppose you mean selling off some of the land next door, do you?"

"Well, something like that...yes. Seems like the obvious move."

"How about insurance?" Dad asked, straight out. "Was the old house insured?"

Bott looked shifty. "I believe so," he grunted.

"Well," said Dad between huge gulps of coffee, "the insurance money could help to pay for a new unit without there being any need to sell the land in a hurry. I'm sure your poor aunts are not fit to be worrying about such things just now, are they? I expect the insurance company will be in touch with you very soon. Anyway, I must be off to work, I'm late—goodbye, everyone! Let me know if I can help in any way, Bottomley." And he beamed at us all and walked out!

I don't know why Dad looked so cheerful, but at least Bott knew he was being watched.

Chapter 22

Mum left work soon after lunch that day, so Sophie and I walked down to the district hospital to visit Violet. We were in time for visiting hours. Mum had seen her earlier, but only for a few minutes. She was being kept "under observation" in hospital for a few days.

"She's still rather shocked and confused," Mum told us, "and she's sedated. She might seem a bit vague when you see her. They say she's suffering from malnutrition, too. I suppose those poor old things have just been living on cups of tea and toast."

Right, I thought, remembering the almost empty pantry at *Featherbys*. It seemed crazy, when the two old ladies could have been quite rich and living on smoked salmon and oysters and chocolate mousse and custard.

Violet was in the corner of a four-bed ward. There were two empty beds and in the fourth lay a very old lady who seemed to be asleep—or maybe dead. She was completely still, just a hump under the covers.

Sophie and I tiptoed in. We weren't used to hospital visiting, and it was embarrassing to find Violet lying there with her eyes closed. People look very private when they are asleep.

"We'd better not wake her up," whispered Sophie.

"She might be just resting," I muttered back.

We stood there feeling silly. Should we cough? Violet looked tiny, sort of shrunk and dried up, under the white sheet. Her hair had been brushed, though, and it was quite pretty with a pale blue bow tied on top.

Just then a nurse bounced in. "Hello, girls!" she said loudly and cheerfully. "Have you come to visit Miss Featherby? That's good—it'll cheer her up. Won't it, Miss Featherby!" She stroked Violet's forehead quite kindly. "Look dear, you've got two visitors!" I wished she wouldn't shout—Violet wasn't deaf. I suddenly realized how noisy the hospital was, full of voices and clatter.

Violet's eyes opened rather vaguely and then focused on us. After a pause she smiled a bit, "Oh—the girls— how nice! Thank you, nurse, I'll sit up higher if you can help me."

The nurse heaved up and pounded the pillows. "There you are, dear. Now, girls, bring a couple of chairs and then you'll all be comfortable." She went and peered at the other ancient patient and felt her pulse. That old lady couldn't have been dead because the nurse didn't ring alarm bells or anything; she just went out and left us alone.

Violet was looking more alive now that her eyes were open.

"How are you feeling?" asked Sophie.

"Not too bad, thank you, Sophie, but I *am* enjoying this rest!"

I bet you are, I thought. Not having to run after Alice all day long and to keep the house going and light the stove. Ouch!—better not mention the stove! Then I was just about to say I was sorry that the house had burnt down, but ouch again—perhaps Violet didn't realize that it had! And perhaps she didn't know about Alice having a heart attack, or anything! We'd have to watch what we said.

"Um...has Mr. Bottomley been to see you?" I asked instead. If Bott had been, he would have told her everything, I bet.

"Mervyn? Yes...he did come in earlier, I think. I've been sleeping such a lot...but that's right, he did come. And, yes, he told me that the house had burnt down. And I remember now, *you* two came knocking on our door to help us that night. It was so good of you all...I could never have managed Alice on my own."

"It was just lucky that Sophie's dad happened to see the glow," I said rather feebly, "and Ben sniffed the smoke." I wondered if Violet would have noticed anything at all before the roof collapsed on top of them?

One of the hospital staff came in with a little tray. "Here's some afternoon tea, love," she said to Violet.

"Oh, thank you!" said Violet. She looked at the cup of tea and the small iced cake as if she were Vicky at a birthday party. "The food here is delicious!" she said. "Such lovely things. I'm not used to being waited on like this—it's delightful!" She lay there peacefully while Sophie helped her with the cup.

We didn't stay much longer because Violet was looking sleepy again, but she asked us to come back next day, so she must have liked seeing us. Alice was too ill to see anybody, we were told.

As we walked home, I said to Sophie, "Violet didn't seem to be upset about the house, did she. Just as well she can't see it!"

"Maybe it's the pills she's on, "said Sophie. "They

could be sort of happy pills. She's certainly happy about lying there and being waited on."

"Well, wouldn't you be, after being Alice's slave for half your life? Poor Violet—I wonder when she last had a holiday or even a rest?"

Mum agreed when we got home, "Yes, it must seem like a huge load has rolled off her back. Someone else is looking after Alice and the house is gone. That's all she can take in at the moment, that *she* isn't responsible for anything, so she's just lying there sleeping and wallowing in luxury. The disaster hasn't really hit her yet."

"It's awful that they were so proud of that old place, or Alice was, but in the end it was like a prison for them really," said Sophie.

"It almost killed them, actually," I pointed out, "first by being such a worry and then by burning down on top of them."

Next day Violet was sitting up in bed. Her mind was clearer but she didn't seem so calm. Her hands were twitching all the time.

"They took me in a wheelchair to see poor Alice," she told us. "She is very ill…I didn't know it was so bad. But her heart has been a trouble for years now."

"Was she able to say anything?" I asked. I tried to sound sympathetic, but of course I was wondering about Alice's will and whether she'd made a new one before the fire.

"Just a little. Oh dear, I'm not sure if she realizes that the house is lost, and no one must say anything yet—another shock would be too much." Her eyes glistened with tears. "I can't believe it myself yet. Does it look dreadful?" Her voice was shuddery.

"Yes, pretty dreadful," said Sophie, "especially at the back, but some of the front walls are left. Mr. Bottomley has been having a few bits of furniture taken away, things that the water didn't spoil. Oh…and Jess saved the portrait in the front room and your photographs."

"You did?" Violet lay back weakly. "That's lovely, Jess. I hadn't even thought that they might have gone— Grandfather's picture…and all those photos." She stared across to the window. "Those were the happy days, but it wasn't a happy house anymore." Suddenly she said, "In a way I'm *glad* it's gone, I'm glad! The fire was meant to happen, I think, to burn up the sadness and the worry."

I wasn't sure if Violet was speaking to us or if she even remembered that we were there. Did she know she'd left the flue open? I glanced at Sophie, who made a face. Violet was still murmuring on.

"Poor Alice—our young days were so happy, then suddenly there was nothing left…Arthur first, then Joyce, Father and Mother, all dead. Only Mervyn now, and he's been such a disappointment to us. Alice did her best to be head of the family. We clung to the old place and to our memories because that was all we had, but they trapped us really, trapped us back there in the past."

"Like a prison?" Sophie asked.

"Yes, in a way, a prison—no longer a happy place."

"What is going to happen to it, do you think?"

Violet looked back at us as if she'd just noticed we were there. She shook her head slowly. "I don't know. Alice said something to me today. She said, 'It's for Arthur now.' I'm not sure that I understand what she meant."

"But Arthur's been dead for fifty years!"

Violet nodded. "Yes, that's why I don't understand."

Chapter 23

Miss Alice died during the night. Mum had rung the hospital next morning for news and was told that Alice had another heart attack in her sleep and had died almost at once. Mr. Bottomley had been notified, the hospital said.

Mum told us the news at breakfast time. It seemed unreal. Alice had been there last night and now she'd gone, and after a few minutes of getting used to the idea we just went on eating toast. If it had been Violet, I would have felt really shocked and weepy, but somehow I didn't feel like that about Alice—and not just because she was an old dragon. It was almost as if she'd died on the night of the fire. She and the old house seemed to be part of one another, and they died together. She *was* like a dragon in one of those old stories, guarding her treasure.

Mum said all those things grown-ups usually say when an old, sick person dies—that it was a blessing and that to die in your sleep is the kindest way, etc., etc. I suppose it was true for Alice.

Sophie said, "I couldn't imagine Alice in a *unit,* could you? And she would have hated to see *Featherbys* now, all black and ruined and horrible."

Sophie and I had wandered in there after we'd heard the news. We weren't supposed to. Dad had said it was dangerous and that Bott could have us up for trespassing, as there was no one living there now, but we didn't care. Vicky was with us, busily washing "Victoria" again, and the boys were at Fontanas' trying to bowl leg spinners. The kids had been solemn for about ten minutes after they'd heard Alice had died, but then they just went on doing their usual things as if nothing had happened.

Sophie and I sat on the ground near the fountain. We had our backs to the burnt-out house because we didn't want to look at it. "Well," I said, "what's going to happen *now?* Everything seems to be working out right for Bott."

"Mmm—it's not fair," sighed Sophie. "And poor Violet, what's she going to do? She can't stay in hospital much longer because there's nothing really wrong with her. She's only there for rest and observation."

"I suppose Bott will get her the unit as soon as possible, but in the meantime…well, he's not going to have her at *his* place."

"Just as well, too!" Sophie sat up. "But, I've been thinking—she could come and stay with us! We've got that little spare room Mum used for sewing and storing junk, but there's a bed in it and I could tidy it up and Violet could stay there until her unit's ready. I'd really like that!"

"What would she do all day while you're at school and everyone's out?"

"She's used to that. She could just rest and get better, and we could feed her up a bit and look after her. Maybe your mum could do something to her hair and see about her clothes! I'll see what Dad and Robbo think."

"Okay—if that works out then there's just one big problem left. What's going to happen to this place?" I looked around at the jungle. Spring had come to the garden, and some of the bulbs we'd uncovered were flowering through the grass and among the white onion bells, and the old roses were making buds. Even the new flowers around the fountain looked bigger. In spite of the ugly ruin behind us, the garden was growing prettier every day.

"Let's turn the fountain on," said Sophie. "Alice would like us to do that, I bet." She went to the tap and soon the water was leaping from the boy's pipe and twinkling in the air. Vicky dropped her scrubbing brush and ran over to the fountain to watch.

"Hi, 'Arthur'!" she called. "How are you today?" Vicky talked to herself a lot and to all her imaginary friends. I suppose it helped her to feel less lonely when Sophie was with me and Robbo was with Ben. There she was, chattering away to the bronze boy on the fountain, and not even noticing us.

Sophie was watching her. "What was it Alice said to Violet—you know, in the hospital before she died? About Arthur?"

"Um, yes...let's think...she said 'It's for Arthur now,' didn't she? And we thought she meant *Featherbys,* and we said Arthur had been dead for fifty years and it didn't make sense."

"Well, don't you see...she could have meant *this* Arthur."

"But he's a statue."

"Yes, but he's more than that—remember what Alice said to Bott that day when he was so beastly about the fountain. She said the boy up there reminded her and Violet of their brother Arthur and it was like a memorial to him. The two Arthurs are sort of the same. When she said 'It's for Arthur now' she could have meant it was to be a memorial—not just the fountain, but the whole place. She didn't say it was 'for Mervyn now,' did she, and we know she didn't want everything to be bulldozed and sold off."

"I suppose she might have meant something like that, or maybe she was just wandering, you know...gaga. We could suggest it to Violet, anyway—but she's probably too upset just now. We'd better wait a bit."

Alice Featherby's funeral was only the second one I'd ever been to, after Mrs. Fontana's. The boys and Vicky didn't go, but Mum said Sophie and I could go if we wanted to, and we thought we would because of Violet. She had no family left, except Bott—and he was useless.

Mrs. Fontana's funeral had been really sad because she was young and everyone had been so upset, but after it was all over it made you feel better, somehow, just because so many people were upset and sad together, and hugging one another and saying lovely things about her. Alice's funeral was much worse because there was hardly anybody there. It was in a chapel at the funeral parlor, with mushy piped music, and it was very quick. After all that long life in Bottlebrush.

Violet sat very small in the front row, with Bott beside her, but he didn't do anything to help her, like holding her hand or lending her his hanky. Not that she cried much. Mum and Dad and Joe Fontana were there, with Sophie and me, but we couldn't sit with Violet because we weren't family. Bott would have been furious if we'd tried. The Jacketts came and so did Uncle Leo, and old Mr. Plumpton turned up, too, with a younger man who was probably his son, the lawyer. Mrs. Rudd from the corner store crept into the back row, and there were a couple of other people I didn't know. Sandra and Bartram were at work, of course, but they'd sent a huge sheaf of purple gladioli. Mum said they clashed with all the other flowers, and she liked the bunch of daisies and honeysuckle Sophie and I had picked from Alice's own garden much better.

Sophie cried a lot, quietly into her handkerchief, but I think it was more for her own mum than for Alice. I tucked my arm through hers and held on.

I tried not to look at the polished coffin up there in front of us, even though it was very splendid with its silver handles. I didn't want to think about Alice being inside that box, so I looked at the floor. The last we'd seen of Alice had been during the fire when our dads had carried her outside to the stretcher. She'd looked halfway dead even then. The real Alice to remember was the fierce old dragon guarding her beloved *Featherbys*. Now she'd gone and she'd left her treasure behind.

Poor Violet was shaky and lost, and Mum drove her back to the hospital soon after the funeral. The doctor had said she could stay on there a bit longer under the circumstances, and Mum said they'd keep her well sedated for a bit. Bott was so busy talking to young Plumpton, the lawyer, about insurance and moving the furniture out and buying the unit, that he didn't notice Dad and old Plumpton out in the parking lot having a very deep conversation. I noticed, but I soon forgot it.

Chapter 24

Sophie and I visited the hospital again the next day. Mum said that Violet had asked to see us. I wondered what I was going to say about Alice, but at least Sophie would be there and Sophie was better at saying things than I was. We took some more flowers out of the old garden, some of the bluebells that had pushed through the grass and some white daisies. I couldn't believe what a difference they made to the shiny, hard ward with its metal beds and spotless floor. The flowers brought a smile to its face.

The old lady in the corner bed was still there and still just a mound, but she was facing the other way now, and a third person was lying in the bed opposite Violet— a fat woman who groaned now and again, just enough to put us off. We could tell she was listening to us, too, although her eyes were shut.

Violet was sitting in a chair and she smiled and made it easy by thanking us for coming and for being at the funeral and for the flowers and everything, and she said that she was really happy for Alice that she'd died quietly like that in her sleep, and that all the worry and illness was at an end for her. We didn't really have to say anything much—thank goodness, with that fat lady eavesdropping!

"And I still mean what I said about the house, that it's better gone," Violet said. "It was such a worry for me. I've wanted to move for a very long time, you know. It was Alice who was determined to stay on, but I don't think she noticed how dilapidated everything had become, not until those last few days at any rate. So, when I feel a little stronger I shall quite enjoy setting myself up in a unit, and the hospital people have suggested that I should get Meals on Wheels and some home help and things like that. Won't that be good!"

"Well, in the meantime," said Sophie rather nervously, "I wonder if you would like to come and stay with us?" She rushed on before Violet could say anything. "I've asked Dad and Robbo and they'd like it, too, and I'd love it—it gets pretty boring with no other girls in the house, and we have a small spare room I could turn back into a bedroom for you, and Jess's mum said she'd take you down to the salon to have your hair done once a week and we could help you to buy some new clothes and things like that."

Violet's eyes were looking red again, so I butted in. "Oh, you'll say yes, won't you—Sophie is looking forward to it such a lot!"

Violet reached out her hand and Sophie took it. "I'll just have to think about it, dear. I hadn't quite realized that I'd have to go somewhere else after this…it all seems so difficult. Oh dear.…I don't think Mervyn could have me in his apartment, so I might very well say yes if you are sure…goodness, people have been so kind."

Then we told her about us sitting by the fountain while Vicky was talking to "Arthur" and how we'd suddenly had this idea that Alice might have meant some sort of memorial when she said that "it was for Arthur now."

"It didn't sound as though she wanted the land to be sold for development," I said, being careful to leave Bott's name out of it.

"Oh no, she certainly didn't want that," said Violet. "We talked about it such a lot in the last few days, just before the fire. I think that was partly why she became ill—all that extra worry, with Mervyn talking about bulldozers and subdivision. Alice was particularly anxious about the oaks, as you know." She sighed. "Anyway, now it's my worry."

Chapter 25

The vacation was rushing to an end. Sophie and I couldn't believe that so much had happened so quickly in our dull old suburban block—the Featherbys, the fountain, the fire, the funeral—and now we had only a few days left, just when we needed loads more time!

"I'd better get the room ready for Violet, anyway," said Sophie. "I think she'll come to stay, don't you? Where else could she go, except to a nursing home or something, and I bet she'd freak out if that happened."

Sophie had told me that actually her dad hadn't been too keen for Violet to move in, but in the end he'd agreed after Uncle Leo had roared at him a bit. "Okay, as long as it's not for too long," he'd said. "I suppose the old duck has to go somewhere."

On Saturday morning I helped Sophie to clear out the Fontanas' spare room. It hadn't really been done properly since Sophie's mum died, and it was rather creepy sorting through things which she'd left behind, like a half-finished shirt that she'd been sewing for Robbo and which was now far too small for him, and all her dress patterns and fabric and some of her own clothes in the cupboard. There was one special red dress that Mrs. Fontana had worn on Christmas Day two years before. I could remember how gorgeous she'd looked with her black hair swirled up on top and her beautiful smile. Sophie burst into tears when she found this dress and I didn't know what we could do about all this stuff, so I went and got Mum.

Mum took one look. "I tell you what, Sophie," she said, "I'll take all these bits and pieces next door so that you can get the room clear for Violet, and we'll sort through them later when there's time." Mum piled everything into a laundry basket and left us to it. Sometimes Mum got it right.

We vacuumed the room clear of dust and cobwebs and polished the window and made up the spare bed with a pink quilt on top. Sophie lugged in a small chair from the living room and found a pink mat to put on the chest of drawers. She was still sniffing a bit. "Violet can have the mirror out of my room," she said, "and I'll use the one in the bathroom. And when...if she comes, I'll do some flowers and put some magazines by the bed."

"Well, be careful which mags you choose—the 1990s are going to be quite a shock to Violet unless we bring her up to date gradually...you know, things like the Internet and heart transplants and global warming might blow her mind! What about a reading lamp?"

"Oh, brainy you...I'll ask Dad to fix one up."

I looked around the room. It seemed a bit empty, somehow, with bare walls. "Don't move—I've just thought of something!" I told Sophie as I dashed off to our place. I came back loaded up with all the Featherby photos and Grandfather's portrait. "Here we have the crowning touch!" I crowed.

"You're brilliant, Jess Huggins." Sophie had recovered and was smiling again. "Let's hang Grandpa on that hook over there where Violet can see him from the chair! He looks pretty stuck-up, doesn't he—I wonder if he really was?"

We hung the old boy on the wall and stood back to check out the effect. "He seems a bit more friendly in this bright room than he did in their gloomy old place," I decided.

Then we sorted through the framed photos. We'd never had a chance to really stare at them because it would have been rude and anyway it had been too dark to see them properly at *Featherbys*. The brightness here showed just how dirty they were.

"I'll get some cleaning stuff," said Sophie, scooting off. She brought rags and silver polish and glass cleaner, and while we rubbed we were able to peer really closely at the faces under the glass. There was a picture of Arthur in his army uniform, looking weirdly young compared to his ancient sisters. It was strange that he never grew old with them, and that when he died his hair was still thick and dark and he hadn't any wrinkles. Arthur had been quite handsome, but he looked very serious—almost as if he were wearing a mask. I suppose he was thinking about the war he was going to. Could he ever have been naughty as a small boy or as maddening as Ben sometimes was?

There was a small photo I hadn't noticed before of another man in uniform. Like Arthur, he looked very serious and well-brushed. "Hello, who's this hero?" I said.

Sophie took it and peered at the face. "Could be Bott's father?"

"Nope—this one's in army uniform. Gerald Bott was air force. Anyway, they wouldn't have kept a photo of *him*—they would have chucked it on the fire!"

"Yeah. Well, he doesn't look like a Featherby anyway."

There were family group photos and ancient weddings and pictures of children and babies in old-fashioned clothes. In some of them we thought we could recognize Alice and Violet as teenagers, if you could call them that.

I polished away at a grimy frame. "Poor things, fancy having to wear those yuk clothes. Alice must have been about our age in this one."

"Imagine Alice in a T-shirt and jeans and Reeboks!" gasped Sophie. I couldn't. It wasn't possible.

The photo we stared at longest was one of Joyce. She looked about twenty, so it was probably taken before she eloped with Bott's father. Joyce had thick waving hair tied loosely behind and a shining smile. Her laughing face made you want to smile back. There was no mask on her face.

"Wasn't she gorgeous!" said Sophie. "She's the only one who looks happy. Let's put her in the front row—that smile deserves it. How awful that everything went wrong for her afterwards."

"You'd never guess that she was Bott's mother, would you?"

Mum was suddenly calling out at the Fontanas' back door. "Can I come in? I've just rung the hospital to see what's what, and Violet can leave tomorrow...they need her bed, anyway. The nurse thinks it would be a great idea to bring her here...so, are you all ready?"

Sophie was beaming again as she led Mum into the spare room. "Come and see, Mrs. Huggins! Will it do?" Mum seemed really amazed. "That's perfect! I think Violet will love it, surrounded by her family portraits." She peered at the photos. Their silver frames were dazzling now and made the tiny room look rich. "Who is *that* raving beauty?" she asked, looking at Joyce. When we'd explained, Mum just said *"Bottomley's* mother! I'd never have guessed! Lucky there isn't one of Bottomley!"

"Oh, don't mention him," I groaned. "Just thinking about him and his bulldozer spoils everything!"

Sophie and I went with Mum next day to collect Violet. Beforehand we had been into *Featherbys* and had picked a bunch of daisies and honeysuckle, which now sat alongside Joyce on the chest of drawers.

Violet had almost no luggage because most of her things had been burnt in the fire. Bott had found some clothes in one of the half-burnt wardrobes, and he had dumped them at the hospital in a carton. Mum had brought them home and washed the things worth saving and these were now hanging up in Violet's new room.

A nurse pushed her out to the car in a wheelchair.

"I don't need this contraption," said Violet, climbing out of it. "They do spoil you here! But I'm not sorry to leave. It will be lovely to go home...with you, Sophie."

I could tell she was going to say "home" meaning *Featherbys*. She still hadn't taken it in that there was no home to go to. We'd decided to drive back to the Fontanas' the longer way so as not to go past *Featherbys*. "There'll be time for that," said Mum. "She can walk in there when she's ready, but let's get her settled in her little pink room first with all her relations in their frames to keep her company."

It was a few days before Violet even asked about *Featherbys*. We were back at school by then, but we'd settled Violet in pretty well by the end of our vacation. She seemed very happy in her new room, and Sophie fussed about like a mother hen...making sure Violet ate enough, sending her early to bed, folding down the pink quilt and taking in cups of tea. Mr. Fontana and Robbo were a bit shy at first about having her there, but soon they were treating her like an ancient aunt and she was teaching them to play card games called Rummy and Bizique.

Robbo wanted to teach her Monopoly, but Sophie grabbed the game from him and stowed it in the top of a cupboard. "You stupid idiot—it's all about buying and selling houses, isn't it! That's the last thing she wants just now when she's doing it for real!"

Violet thanked us several times for rescuing her photos and polishing them up. One day I put on my casual voice and asked her who the other soldier was, the one in the small frame. Violet picked him up and gazed at his solemn face.

"He was a friend...of the family. Neville, his name was. He went away, too, like Arthur."

"What happened?" I coaxed.

"He was wounded, escaping from Greece—not too badly, thank goodness—but we never saw him again. After the war he stayed over there, in England. He wrote once then, to say he was married." Violet's voice faded and I had a sudden feeling about this man who had left his photograph behind. Would *Violet* have married him if he hadn't gone to the war? I couldn't ask her that, but I noticed that she'd put his photo in the front row beside Joyce's. Poor Violet, he'd married someone else and was probably dead by now, but she still gazed at his photo after fifty years!

On the last day of our holidays Mum took Violet to the Bottlebrush Hair Salon and gave her the full treatment, cutting and shampooing her hair and giving it a light rinse and a perm to fix the straggles. Mum's a genius! Violet looked about twenty years younger without her wispy bun.

Then Sophie and I escorted her across to Annabelle's Fashions. Annabelle was really Mrs. Bird, and while Sophie and Violet were looking around, I hissed to Mrs. Bird not to show Violet any dreary geriatric fashions in black or gray.

"No way, Jess," Mrs. Bird agreed behind the coat rack. She peered through the coats at Violet. "Yes, pink or blue for her, I think. Leave it to me!"

An hour later Violet had bought a blue dress, a deep-pink two-piece outfit, a couple of cardigans to mix and match, some nighties and a soft cream dressing gown, and she'd opened an account. It must have felt to her like starting a new life or a holiday, and I suppose for a few days she just pushed *Featherbys* out of her mind.

We had other things to think about, too, mainly school. Going back to school was like dragging myself out of bed after a long, exciting dream, and I wanted the dream to go on because it wasn't finished yet. School was a nuisance, so I was in a bit of a bad mood that afternoon when Sophie came dashing in from next door.

"Are you home, Jess?" she called. "The dreaded moment has come—Violet wants to go and look at *Featherbys!* She's waited for us to get home so that we can take her in. It's going to be awful, I think, when she sees the ruins."

Chapter 26

From the Fontanas' place you would never have known that there'd been a fire at *Featherbys* because of the great wall of trees. Even the burnt stench had gone at last. Violet hadn't asked any questions about the fire since that day in hospital.

I said to Sophie, "I hope she won't be too shattered. She can't have any idea how horrible it looks."

"No...it'll be like looking at a dead person," said Sophie.

Violet wanted to walk around to *Featherbys* and go in by the front gate. She was all dressed up in her new pink outfit with a straw hat, which Mum had lent her, and she had a walking stick. She could have been going to a tea party.

We set off from the Fontanas' front gate, past our place. That way was the furthest from the ruins.

"That's where the Pyles live," I told Violet as we passed their house. The 4-wheel drive and the boat were parked at the side, spotless and gleaming. "You know, the people who want to buy some of your land."

"Yes, yes, I remember," snapped Violet. "For a garage." I'd never heard Violet snap before, not while Alice was alive. Alice had done the snapping for both of them.

We rounded the corner and walked along the side street, where the great Featherby oaks spread over the hedge and the yard was a tangle of long shaggy grass and rubbish. We turned into the far street and reached the front gate of *Featherbys*. This side was just as untidy and overgrown. Luckily the privet flowers weren't out yet or we would have sneezed ourselves inside out.

Violet stopped for a minute and leaned on her stick. "Well, here we are. Just let me get my breath."

I think we all had the jitters.

"All right—in we go, girls. Lead the way," she told us, and I opened the squeaky gate and pushed aside the overhanging privet while she walked through to see what had happened to her old home.

We couldn't really see the house from the gate because of the jungle, and Violet stopped to stare at the honeysuckle, which was seething with bees. "Smell it!" she exclaimed, "and see those old roses rambling over the tree!"

Even our feeble efforts at weeding and tidying had helped a bit…there were daisies poking through the grass, and the flowers around the fountain were growing fast in their chicken manure and already pushing up buds. The garden basked in the warm sun and "Arthur" stood gleaming on his pedestal. This had been a good way to come in.

Violet gripped her stick and walked on slowly until she reached the fountain. Then she stood and looked at the ruined, roofless house beyond the two scorched trees. Its empty windows stared back at her through their black smudgy frames.

Sophie was right—for Violet this must have been like seeing the battered dead body of someone she'd known all her life. She'd lived in that house for about eighty years, with her mum and dad, and Joyce and Arthur, and servants, as well as all those years alone with Alice. She could remember it in the happy days, but in hospital she'd told us that it was no longer a happy house and that she was glad it had gone. Would she still feel glad now that she was looking at its corpse?

We stood beside Violet and I hoped she wouldn't faint or anything. I was brilliant with sprained ankles, but not much good with swoons. There wasn't even anywhere for her to sit. She looked at the house for a long time, and a sort of shudder went through her as she leaned on her stick. Then she said, "Well, the fire did a thorough job, didn't it....I didn't realize...come on, I'd better see it all. Can we go around the back?"

We helped her around the side along one of our little trails, past the bush where Sophie and I had eavesdropped on the Pyles. The wreckage of the kitchen lay there, and Violet made a sort of crying noise when she saw it. "There's nothing left!" she whispered.

It had rained a bit since the fire and a few relics were showing up in the ashes, like a metal door knob and a broken cup. The battered kettle was still on the stove.

"There's the teapot!" Sophie pointed. "It's not even cracked." It was wedged beside a piece of crumpled roofing iron, but there was no sign of its lid.

"Mother used to pour tea from that pot," Violet whispered. "I'd like to have it, if we can find the lid." She was shaking and very white, but she wasn't fainting, thank goodness.

I rescued the old pot. Its glaze was crusty with gray ash but that looked as if it would wash off. Sophie began poking about with a stick, and together we gingerly lifted up the sheet of iron and scratched about in the ashes, and to our surprise we found the lid quite quickly.

"It's got a bit of a chip on the underneath," frowned Sophie.

"Oh, but that was there already! It doesn't matter at all! Alice chipped it once on the kitchen tap." Violet was smiling now as she fitted the lid onto the pot. "There now, see! When it's scoured, you'll never know. Oh, I am so pleased we found it. Thank you, girls. Now I think I've seen quite enough, and I'd like to sit down and get used to the idea."

We helped her home to the Fontanas' and she went to bed very early that night.

Chapter 27

Violet stayed in bed in the mornings, resting, and long after the Fontanas had all gone to work or school she would get up slowly and make some breakfast. After the first few days she began to do little jobs to help Sophie, like washing the breakfast things and peeling veggies for the evening.

She also had visitors. She asked the Fontanas if they minded, and of course they didn't, and Joe said she could use the front room and the telephone because he knew she'd have a lot of things to sort out about *Featherbys*.

Some of the people who came were old Mr. Plumpton and young Mr. Plumpton, the lawyer, and someone from the insurance company. A man from the town council went to inspect the ruins of the old house and said the walls were unsafe and would have to be demolished.

Bott came several times, we guessed, although Violet didn't tell us much, but she did say that he was making arrangements to buy the unit for her as soon as the insurance money came through. Sophie and I wondered what other "arrangements" Bott was making. We felt nervous when another sheaf of flowers was delivered to Violet with a typed card saying, *Our deepest commiserations, Bartram and Sandra Pyle. (Do let us know if we can help in any way.)*

"Like chopping down your oaks, that means," I muttered.

Dad visited Violet several times and when we asked him what was going on he just said, "Oh, this and that...you know, business arrangements," which made Sophie and me mad. Why do adults get all secretive about these things? We were just as involved as everyone else, but nobody would tell us anything and we were worrying ourselves to shreds waiting for Bott and his bulldozer to appear.

I even had a nightmare. The whole garden at *Featherbys* was on fire and Violet was trying to put it out, scooping water from the fountain with her old tin bucket. Alice was standing by the gate puffing out smoke, and she had green claws like a dragon and fierce red eyes in her white face. There were no bulldozers, but Bott was up above in a hot-air balloon, slurping a cup of tea. I was trying to get through the fence to help Violet, but I couldn't find the gaps—they'd all been boarded up and there were no footholds to help me over. I was so desperate that I woke and found myself all wound up in the sheet!

And then early one morning thunderous noises from *Featherbys* made me rocket out of bed—roaring truck noises, shouts, thumps, and crashes.

"What's happening?" I yelled through the house. "Is it Bott? Is he knocking it all down? The fountain and the trees and everything?"

Dad was shaving and looked out of the bathroom with a soapy face. "For heaven's sake, Jess, stop yelling! It'll be the demolition chaps—they've come to knock down the walls and cart the rubble away. Those old walls are dangerous, you know—Miss Violet asked Joe to arrange it all for her."

"Why didn't someone tell us? How do you know they won't start wrecking the garden?"

"Because Miss Violet gave instructions that they were not to touch anything else. They're working from the back, where the fire engines were, just clearing away the ruins and cleaning up that area." Dad patted my shoulder, and a dollop of shaving soap splotted onto the carpet. "Go along—get dressed and stop worrying. It's going to be all right."

On my way to school I detoured into the side street to have a look. There were two massive dump trucks drawn up to the fence, and the demolition men were crashing sheets of twisted iron into one of them, while another man was zooming about in a big Bobcat scooping up piles of bricks and stuff and tipping them into the other truck. The noise was terrible and so was the swirling dust and grit, so I escaped to school. I'd wanted to ask the men to rescue anything that showed up in the ashes, like the teapot we'd saved. Maybe there were other things there like cups and plates—but it was hopeless. I couldn't make myself heard or even noticed above the din and dust. What was the use? They wouldn't be bothered with that sort of thing, anyway, with their great smashing machines.

It took them several days to finish the job, and on the last day, after school, all five of us kids crept through the hole in the fence to have a look. The boys had been there on the afternoon when the old brick chimneys had toppled down, and they were excited by all the roaring machinery and noise. But on this day, as we went through the jungle, there was silence, and as we pushed aside the branches and reached the old yard, or where the yard had been, we found ourselves staring at emptiness.

Where *Featherbys* had stood there was nothing except bare ashy earth, all raked flat and tidy. Even the sheds had gone and the gap in the hedge was blocked up. The ruins and rubble had been awful, but at least they were the remains of the old house. This seemed much worse because there wasn't one thing left to show that a house had ever been there or that Featherbys had lived there for a hundred years and had ridden ponies and picked fruit and made jam in the kitchen and had dinner at the big table with the brown cloth. It was creepy and I felt sort of empty.

The boys patrolled around the edge of the gray space, trying to work out where different things had been—the front hall, the kitchen, the stove, the back step where Violet had fallen.

Sophie shivered. "I hope Violet won't want to look—it's horrible. Brrr....I can almost feel Featherby ghosts prowling in the garden, as if they've been disturbed and upset."

She was right...there was a prickling feeling in the air. Around the empty space crowded the trees and the creepers, with Grandfather's oaks looming, as if waiting for something to happen.

Vicky ran off to see if "Arthur" and "Victoria" were safe. It looked as if the demolition gang had obeyed Violet's orders and not touched the garden, but we went to check in any case.

We heard Vicky squeal. "The fountain's on! It's sprinkling!"

Then a man's voice said, "Hello, young lady!" and as we skirted around our eavesdropping bush we saw Mr.

and Mrs. Jackett sitting on folding chairs and having cups of tea from a thermos.

"Well, here are *all* the young people—that's a comfort," said Mrs. Jackett. "And I do believe there's some cake left in the tin, so help yourselves—here," and she handed the tin to Ben, who seized the biggest slice, of course. The garden felt more friendly again.

"What's happening?" asked Robbo. "Why are you having a picnic here?"

Mr. Jackett had a big gulp of tea. "It's a good place for a picnic, don't you reckon? But it was Miss Violet who asked us to come—she wanted someone to keep an eye on the place while all *that* rumpus was going on." He waved towards the gray space. "We didn't want them wrecking more than they had to, did we, or carting any extras away."

Mrs. Jackett nodded.

"You've been looking after 'Arthur' and 'Victoria'!" squealed Vicky. "I'm glad you did. I would have done it, but I had to go to school."

"Yes, and your stone seats and the sundial and all the trees—we looked after them, too," said Mrs. Jackett, pouring more tea.

"And as soon as all the clearing was done, I turned on the fountain," said Mr. Jackett. "It watered the seedlings and it made us feel better."

We watched the water sparkling from "Arthur's" pipe. "Look," said Sophie, "the first flower has come out in the fountain bed. The ones we planted. A pink one—Miss Alice said they used to be pink and white."

"So they will be," grunted Jackett. "They'll be just the same."

A car door slammed in the street and next thing there, believe it or not, was Mervyn Bottomley marching down the drive towards us, just as he did on the day of the turning-on ceremony! His face was the color of Mum's chili sauce. Why did he always barge in at the wrong moment?

"All right, what's going on?" he demanded. "Don't you know you're trespassing?"

"Of course we're not trespassing, Mr. Bottomley," said Mrs. Jackett calmly. "We're here at Miss Violet's request, just to keep an eye on things during the demolishment. You can ask her if you like—she's still the owner, you know." She gave him a sharp look. "And I'm sorry I can't offer you some tea, but the thermos is empty." She held it upside down to prove it and then handed Robbo the last piece of cake.

That fixed old Bott. He seemed to be looking for something to say; then he noticed the fountain. "Why is that stupid thing on? It's wasting water—if I'd had my way it would have been flattened with everything else!"

He glared at "Arthur" and Vicky shrieked, "No! Miss Violet wants him to stay—we all do!"

"Huh! It's got nothing whatever to do with you lot!" he snorted and strode off to inspect the empty space.

"Look at him," sniffed old Mr. Jackett. "Just can't wait, can he!"

Through the tangle of trees we could see Bott up there, at first pacing about—but then he stopped and stood staring at the space and up at the trees. Were the Featherby ghosts crowding around him, too? Everything was hushed except for the sprinkling water.

Chapter 28

That evening Mum was late in from work so Dad brought home some take-out food that was lukewarm-greasy and not a great hit. "It's time we had another proper dinner," said Mum, poking about on her plate. "How about Saturday evening? I know—we'll ask the Fontanas to bring Violet in and we'll have a celebration."

Ben stared at her. "Mum! Violet's sister's just died and her house burnt down—so what's there to celebrate, hey?"

"Yes, Ben, I hadn't forgotten," sighed Mum, "but at least we can make her feel welcome and try to cheer her up. You know what I mean."

Ben was too thick to work out that Violet not being burnt to death could be something to celebrate. In any case Mum and Dad had a silly look on their faces, that trying-not-to-smile look that meant they were sitting on something. I pretended not to notice and said, "Well, as long as you don't cook up one of your Mexican dynamite recipes, Mum. Violet's digestive system wouldn't survive."

"I'd thought of a plain chicken casserole with scalloped potatoes and steamed broccoli, followed by strawberry mousse," sniffed Mum. "Will that pass?"

"Sure, that sounds safe enough." I *knew* it—Mum had this thing all planned—down to the steamed broccoli.

It wasn't just an urge to have a dinner party at all.

When I told Sophie, she agreed that something was cooking and it wasn't just chicken casserole.

When Saturday came we had to put the extra leaf in the dining table so that ten of us could fit around it. Uncle Leo Fontana had been invited, too. Mum said I could arrange the seating.

"Put me at one end and Dad at the other," she said, "and Violet should be on Dad's right as the special guest."

"Who'll be on your right?"

"Probably Uncle Leo, with Joe on my left."

Well, there didn't seem to be much arranging left for me to do, as Mum had most of it worked out, as usual, but I filled in the other places. Starting with Dad and going around, the seating went: Violet, Robbo, me, Joe Fontana, Mum, Uncle Leo, Vicky on a cushion, Ben, and Sophie on Dad's left.

Mum dragged out her best dinner set and gave it a thorough wipe, as we hadn't used it since last Christmas. Vicky helped, sort of, by putting around the knives and forks and spoons. She took hours to get them straight and even then half of them were back-to-front. When they were sorted out, the table looked really classy all set up like that.

Without being told to we all made a special effort to dress up, even though this was supposed to be just a Saturday casserole meal and nothing out of the ordinary. But there was a sort of zing in the air. All the men wore ties and the boys combed their hair down sleek with water, while Vicky's braids were festooned with huge white bows. I borrowed a narrow pink scarf from Mum to brighten up my mousy hair, and Mum said I could wear makeup, too, but not to overdo it.

I did a double take when Sophie came in at the front door because her long black hair was swirled up on top and for a moment I thought it was her mother. It was almost like having a ghost from the past among us. I heard Mum gasp, too.

Violet wore her new blue dress and we all whooped and shrieked at the general glamour. The evening had begun well, and by the time we sat down at the table I was feeling hyped-up and ready for something to happen.

What a letdown! The adults all gassed on about the next elections and soccer and the price of gasoline, and I missed most of it anyway because I was busy helping Mum to serve the meal, which took ages with ten people. *Featherbys* wasn't even mentioned, although Uncle Leo asked Violet about her new unit—but she didn't have much to say about that because she hadn't even seen it yet!

By the time we each had a dish of strawberry mousse in front of us and the conversation had turned to a new bus service, I'd decided that Sophie and I had been wrong—this wasn't a special occasion at all, but just dinner like Mum said. I wasn't close enough to Sophie to kick her under the table, but we did beam a few desperate looks between us that meant, "What's going on? Aren't adults a lot of pinheads!"

We were just finishing second helpings of mousse when the doorbell rang and Violet let out a startled "Oh!" Violet was very jumpy.

Dad stood up. "It's all right—that will be the Jacketts. I'll let them in." Nobody had told *us* the Jacketts were coming.

Mum said, "Well, if everyone has finished, let's go into the living room and have some coffee in there."

"Do we *have* to?" groaned Ben. "Can't Robbo and I go outside? We don't drink coffee."

"Go out for five minutes then and let off some of that steam," agreed Mum, "but come back in. Miss Violet especially wants you all to be there, don't you, dear."

The old lady nodded. "I do—I want all you children to come in, oh yes."

This seemed more hopeful. I suppose it made sense that we'd waited for the Jacketts to arrive before anything happened—*if* it was going to.

Sophie and I helped Mum to hand round the coffee and tea. The adults were still cackling like cockatoos about the weather and Mr. Jackett's tomato plants and Uncle Leo's new lawn mower. And there was Mrs. Jackett telling Violet about a ginger cake she'd made that had sunk in the middle, as though she was reporting a severe earthquake. It was unbelievable!

It seemed to take forever to settle everyone down on chairs. Dad had to bring in extra ones from the dining room as there were twelve people by now. Mum was topping up the coffee cups and telling Vicky to pass the sugar around, and Sophie and I sank down on the floor in a dark corner and poked one another.

"I can't stand this much longer!" I groaned. The room was as full as a beehive. Then the boys came steaming in. Ben pulled Robbo onto the floor and whispered something to him about "sitting down on his Bottomley." I glared at them furiously to make them behave. Bottomley was the last name we wanted mentioned just now.

Chapter 29

At *last* Dad took charge and welcomed everybody. I don't suppose he included us Hugginses, because we lived there, but he welcomed all the others and especially Miss Violet Featherby. "She has been a neighbor of ours for a long time," he said, "but it is only in the past few weeks that we have become close neighbors, owing to a series of events that have had a devastating effect on Miss Violet's life and that have affected us all."

It was weird to hear Dad making a fancy speech in his own living room, quite embarrassing really, and I was glad to be in the dark corner. Actually Dad was quite good at it, but I suppose being on the Bottlebrush Council gave him plenty of practice. He didn't say much more about the devastating events, which was just as well because Violet was very wobbly.

On he went. "We know that Miss Violet has been under a great strain, but there is something she wants you all to know and she has asked me to speak for her."

Violet was looking very tiny and anxious in her chair and her hands were shaking, but she gave Dad a little smile and said, "Thank you, yes."

I had a nervous stitch in my middle. I elbowed Sophie rather hard. This was it!

"Since the fire, Miss Violet has had many discussions with Mr. Plumpton senior and with me about the future of the property next door. And Mr. Plumpton had already talked to Miss Alice before the fire, so he was aware of *her* thoughts on the matter. I was called in because of my position on the Town Council, and of course young Plumpton, the family lawyer, has been involved as well. In a way, the destruction of the old house in the fire has made a decision much easier."

"What decision?" croaked Ben desperately, and for once I felt like giving Ben a cheer. Dad must have suddenly remembered that he wasn't addressing a public meeting but just a small bunch of friends and family, including wriggling kids.

"Okay, Ben, let's cut it short. Miss Violet has decided that she wants *Featherbys* to be left to the people of Bottlebrush, and she wants it left as a public garden. She has offered it to the Town Council for a very low price on condition that the garden is to be restored, preserving as many of the original features as possible, such as the fountain and the oaks and the best of the other trees and so on."

"And 'Victoria'?" whispered Vicky.

"Of course, dear," said Violet. Now that the news was out, Violet was pink again. The beehive began to buzz, and Uncle Leo was clapping and roaring out "Bravo!" as though he were at the opera. Sophie and I nudged furiously. Then Violet raised her bony little hand for silence.

"I would like to have *given* the old place to the Council," she said, "but I have to sell it because I'll need something to live on when I move into my unit, and to pay expenses, you know. I mustn't be a burden on anyone."

"Of course not, Miss Violet," gasped Mrs. Jackett. "I think you are being ever so generous as it is, when you think what the land is really worth!"

What about BOTT? Sophie was mouthing silently at me. I was squirming with curiosity, too—had Bott been told? But Dad was still standing in his speechifying pose, and we all had to quieten down again while he droned on. "Well, I was in a position to know that the Council's policy is to create more green space and parkland in this locality, so I put Miss Violet's proposal forward for discussion when she first suggested it...."

I felt my eyes glazing over. Dad was in public-meeting mode again. Bott's red face kept flashing through my mind, so I switched on again in time to hear Dad say, "...full Council meeting four nights ago the offer was accepted unanimously and Miss Violet's conditions have also been accepted in principle, although a lot of detailed decisions have yet to be made—for example, what to do with the privet hedge!"

"Huh!" growled Mr. Jackett. "A public garden should be open for the public to *see,* and anyways that privet stinks. Dig it up!" He held out his cup for more tea.

"Quite right, Jackett," said Violet.

Dad cleared his throat and told us to treat the matter as confidential. I suppose if he hadn't been making a speech, he would have told us to keep our traps shut.

Then Violet took over. She had stopped shaking. "I wanted you people to be the first to know because I have so much to thank you all for. You saved us from the fire that night and now you are looking after me like one of your own family. But as well, you have begun to bring the old garden back to life—especially you children. Alice and I had almost lost sight of its beauty under the burden of its upkeep and the worry about its future. That's why I decided that the people of Bottlebrush should have this garden for themselves instead of losing it all for a parking lot or a row of buildings."

"Well, I think it's all just marvelous," said Mum to Violet. "Wouldn't your grandfather be amazed to see his oaks now, surrounded by streets and houses, but still growing. And think of all the people who will sit under them and have picnics when the garden is finished. Harry," she said to Dad, "I think a plaque should be put up on one of the trees, explaining who Grandfather Featherby was and when he planted them. You must write down as much information as you can, Miss Violet...so that Bottlebrush will always remember one of its first families."

"Oh, I'll try, and I would certainly like the fountain to be in my brother's memory," said Violet, "so that people will know that he lost his life in that awful war, in North Africa. The Arthur Featherby Memorial—yes, that's what I'd like it to be, and Alice would have agreed."

A fountain seemed to me like a good memorial for someone who'd died in a desert—I would tell Violet that one day when we were by ourselves. I suppose she'd already thought of it.

Everyone was jabbering again, twice as hard as before, but at least they were all talking about *Featherbys* now. The boys had crawled over to our corner.

"Well...that's one in the eye for Bott," I said to Sophie. "Do you think he knows yet?"

"I'll ask Violet," said Ben, and before we could stop him he went over to her.

"Does Mr. Bottomley know about all this yet?" Ben asked, straight out.

Violet sighed. "No, he doesn't. He's coming to see me tomorrow. I know I should have told him, as he is my only relative, but somehow I had to tell you first and have you all behind me, otherwise I wouldn't be strong enough to stand up to him."

"Won't he get anything?" asked Robbo. After Violet had died is what he meant.

"Oh, of course he will! When I'm gone he'll inherit my unit and whatever money is left and I'll be glad for him to have that...he's my sister's son, after all, and the last of the family. But I think it is *Featherbys* that he really wants."

"Not for itself, though," said Sophie. "Only for the money he could sell it for."

"Yes, I'm afraid that's it. Alice and I have tried to preserve the family heritage to hand on, but Mervyn doesn't have that family loyalty...perhaps it's not his fault. So I hope I've made the right decision—to let *Featherbys* live on as a family memorial and give pleasure to many people at the same time." Violet's hands were shaking again. "Mervyn is going to be very upset, I'm afraid."

"Upset" wasn't the word I'd have chosen—he'd be more like a raging bull!

Chapter 30

Sophie and Robbo were ordered to come to our place on Sunday after lunch, and Joe vanished into his toolshed so that Violet could have the house to herself when Bott arrived. Sophie and I were pretty mad that we couldn't be there to keep an eye on things.

"Can't we wait in the next room in case Violet needs us?" I pleaded with Dad. "Bott is going to go berserk when he finds out about *Featherbys,* and he might attack her with a hammer or something!"

"Heavens, Jess!" shrieked Mum, "I don't think he's *that* crazed...."

"No, we must all keep out of the way," announced Dad in a voice that meant no argument. "It's not our business and it would only antagonize Bottomley even more if any of us were hanging around."

I must have looked worried because Dad ruffled my hair. "Don't worry, Jess—I've made sure that young Plumpton will be there. It's quite in order for Miss Violet to have her lawyer with her, you know. He'll be able to handle it. Lawyers are quite used to this sort of thing."

Mum sniffed. "Yes—they grow rich on cases like this, with people squabbling over property and possessions. It's all very stupid, really. I think Violet has made a very sensible decision, so let's hope Bottomley will see reason...although, with that fiery complexion of his, I have my doubts!"

When the time came, Sophie and I sat on our front verandah as near as possible to the Fontanas' fence, just in case we could hear something from their front room, which was quite close. Maybe Violet would start screaming for help and we could be first on the scene to rescue her from the enraged Bott. Our position on the verandah was screened by a big thick bush at the end.

The boys were sulking because they couldn't play cricket in our dahlia-ridden backyard, especially when Mum was home with both eagle eyes open. They were hanging about, but I could tell they were listening in case of exciting developments next door. Vicky, thank heavens, was out at another birthday party. All her friends seemed to be turning six one after the other, like catching chicken pox.

What on earth was going on in the Fontanas' living room? Through the bush we'd seen young Plumpton arrive, with a fat briefcase. Then Bott stumped in five minutes later. I expected an explosion of angry shouting at any minute, but we couldn't hear a thing.

"I bet the lawyer will take ages to explain things," groaned Sophie. "They always do."

"Yeah, Dad was bad enough last night, making his speech. I thought he'd never get to the point!"

Sophie sank down in her chair. "Oh well, I don't suppose we're missing much really. We know what the lawyer will say because we heard it all last night."

"But what will Bott say or do? *That's* what we're missing out on!" I jigged up and down with frustration. "Still, it's odd...he doesn't seem to be shouting so far—I can usually hear roaring noises from inside your place—you know, when Robbo goes mental or something."

Mum peered out through the wire door. She was looking towards the Fontanas'. "Is everything okay?" she called in a loud whisper.

"We can't hear anything," I hissed back.

Mum nodded and disappeared. Violet's meeting had been going on for well over half an hour.

"Maybe Bott has strangled them," I said, "although I suppose he couldn't strangle them both at once, so one of them would have been able to call for help...."

Sophie stared at me and sat up. "You have a wild imagination, Jess Huggins! You've turned Bott into a raving monster! He's really quite ordinary...and actually, I feel a bit sorry for him."

"*Sorry? Why?*"

"Oh, I don't know—maybe he *is* rude and bad-tempered and not a bit tactful, but it sounds as if he's had a pig of a life. Well, just think...his mum and dad didn't get on, and then she died when he was just a kid, and it must have been awful for him when she was so sick. Then there's been this stupid feud with the Featherbys ever since. He hasn't got any family of his own—there's only Violet left now—and Alice was always jumping on him. You know what she was like—just as rude as Bott in her own way. She almost treated him as if he was still a kid. Maybe he really *was* trying to help them by moving them into a unit. But they just didn't seem able to talk to one another without flying into a rage. Like Mrs. Jackett said, their minds were poisoned."

Sophie is always much kinder about people than I am, but I wasn't too sure about this be-kind-to-Bott notion. Still, I suppose he could have felt a "black empty space" inside him when his mother died, like Sophie did, and I had to admit that Bott had been quite a help to Violet in buying the new unit—but was that for her sake or for his?

"I wish we knew more about Bott's father," I said, "You know, Gerald Bottomley. Nobody seemed to like him."

"He didn't teach Bott any manners, that's for sure!" giggled Sophie. "Still, Bott might get on better with Violet now she's by herself. She's more sympathetic. Alice was always so snooty to him. I don't blame him for losing his temper sometimes, especially with her. After all, the feud wasn't his fault."

I looked at Sophie. *"You've* changed your tune a lot, haven't you!"

"Well, I've been thinking about him a bit and wondering why he's like he is. I bet he's lonely. And I think he's probably jealous of us because we get on better with his Auntie Violet than he does."

I hadn't even thought of that. You don't expect ancient men of fifty to be jealous of kids like us, but maybe Sophie was right. She seemed to understand people much better than I did...and here was I planning to be a famous novelist! If Sophie wanted to write a novel she wouldn't even need to invent a new name. Sophia Fontana had a best-seller ring to it.

I heard a sound next door and I swiveled around to the bush. Young Mr. Plumpton was leaving! He walked quickly down the path, and after a minute we saw his sleek white car zoom off. Violet and Bott were alone in there—this could be red alert!

"Plumpton's gone!" I hissed. "I don't think he was meant to leave before Bott did...what'll we do? D'you think I'd better get Dad?"

"Shush," said Sophie. "Just listen."

We strained our ears and almost stopped breathing. Still no sound.

"Well, she's not screaming or being chased around the room," grinned Sophie, and somehow I felt stupid.

But now there really was a noise. The Fontanas' front door was opening again and our eyes bored through the bush to see Bott heading down the path to the gate, and Violet was with him! He opened the gate and then the door of his car, and slowly Violet climbed in. Bott got into the driver's seat, did a noisy U-turn, and they vanished.

"Where on earth...? Do you think he's kidnapped her?" I found myself saying.

"Jess Huggins!" Sophie exploded. "She wasn't exactly bound up in ropes, was she...and she'd had time to put on her straw hat!"

I rushed inside. "Bott has taken Violet away in his car," I announced to Dad, who was once more poring over his paperwork and clicking away on his laptop.

"Mmmm?" he asked vaguely. "Where to?"

"Well, how do *we* know? We weren't allowed to be there, were we!" Sometimes I felt like hitting him with a cushion.

Mum had joined us in the den by now. "What's happening?"

Sophie giggled again. "Well, Jess thinks Bott might have kidnapped Violet. They've gone off in his car together, but...Bott did open the car door for her—you know, he didn't push her savagely or gag her or anything—and she *had* put her hat on."

I felt a flush surging across my face. Dad pressed the *Save* key and took off his glasses. "Really, Jess—why on earth would Bottomley want to kidnap his aunt in broad daylight? What possible reason could he have? You've just worked yourself into a silly state over all this."

"Yes, dear," agreed Mum. "Just because Bottomley is a disagreeable fellow, that doesn't make him a thug. There is sure to be a perfectly simple explanation."

"I bet they've gone to look at the new unit," said Sophie. "Violet hasn't even seen it yet." Trust Sophie. Why didn't I think of that?

Chapter 31

There was nothing to stop us going into Fontanas' place now. The meeting was over and the house was empty. The boys had already taken over the backyard with their delayed cricket game, after a quick race through the house to see if there were signs of anything interesting—like bloodstains, I suppose, fools.

Sophie and I looked around the house for more sensible clues. There was a small tray on the kitchen sink and on it three used cups and saucers and Mother Featherby's shiny teapot, which Sophie and Violet had soaked and polished and sterilized after we'd rescued it from the fire. Sophie said Violet loved to use it for afternoon teas in spite of its chipped lid.

"Well, they all had a cup of tea," I said, "and some cookies." There were crumbs on a bare plate.

The living room was tidy. "It's just as I left it," said Sophie. "See,"she grinned, "there's no sign of a struggle—no chairs tipped over or smashed vases...hey, but look on that table, Violet's photo album and some of the portraits!" There was the one of Arthur in uniform and a family group with baby Arthur in frills.

"She must have been showing them to Bott," I said. "I bet he wasn't interested. I wonder why she didn't show him the picture of his mother? That's the best of the lot."

Joe Fontana's head came around the door with eye-brows raised like question marks. "Is it all over?" he asked. "Where's everyone, have they gone?"

"Yes, all of them—even Violet's gone out. We think she's gone to look at her unit, with Bott," said Sophie.

Sophie was right, of course. Violet returned after about an hour. Bott brought her to the door but he didn't come in—he just hurried back to his car and drove off. Violet sank onto a chair and took off her hat.

"My goodness, I'm worn out!" she gasped, but her eyes were happy. "Mervyn took me to see my unit, and young Mr. Plumpton met us there too just to check things over."

Sophie's stare bored holes in me. *So much for being kidnapped,* was what she was signaling across the room. I pretended not to notice and asked Violet if she liked the unit.

"Oh yes, it's a ducky little place," she smiled. "No, not little really, but after *Featherbys* it seems so. There are two bedrooms, and such a pretty bathroom, all pink and cream. And there's a bright kitchen with gadgets. I'm glad it's so close—you'll be able to walk around and teach me how to use some of them—and the new stove! I'm sure I won't understand it."

The old black stove with its fizzing kettles and its roaring flue drifted into my mind, but Violet went on.

"I still have to choose carpets and some curtains for the living room, but then it will all be ready. And Mervyn has a few pieces of the old furniture in store for me—some smaller things that were saved by the firemen...a few chairs and Alice's desk and two little tables, and so on."

I didn't want to hear all this, not just now. What had happened about *Featherbys?* That was the question. Why hadn't Bott exploded into a fury? Perhaps Violet had chickened out and not even told him. Dad would say it wasn't our business, but I had to know, after all this suspense.

"Um...what did Mr. Bottomley...er...say about *Featherbys?*" I asked nervously. "We thought he might have been upset."

Violet nodded. She didn't seem to mind me asking. "Well, so did I, but it was remarkable really—he seemed almost *relieved* when Mr. Plumpton explained my scheme. Actually I started off by saying that I wanted the two of us to be friends, as we are the only ones left in the family and it seemed foolish to carry on with the old nonsense, which was not of our making anyway. Well, he didn't say much to that, but he didn't object—I don't suppose he could object, really. So then I let Mr. Plumpton explain about *Featherbys,* and do you know what Mervyn said? He just said, "And a good riddance, too. That place is a millstone around our necks."

"But what about the money?" I asked.

"That didn't seem to concern him greatly, rather to my surprise, although I think he was pleased to know that I'd be leaving the unit to him and anything else that remained. But it just seemed that he had a hatred for the old house and all that it stood for. He certainly didn't want to live there."

I remembered Violet saying in hospital that it was no longer a happy house and she was glad it was gone, so that made two of them.

"Maybe he felt that while you were still living there, the feud would never end," said Sophie. "Now you can forget it."

"Maybe. Poor Mervyn, he's not very good at expressing himself. He's always on the defensive and that makes it hard to get close to him, and I'm afraid Alice never really understood him at all. I don't suppose any of us did."

The old album on the table caught my eye. "Were you showing him the photos?" I asked.

"Yes, when I was explaining about having the garden restored by the Council, I wanted to show the two of them some snaps of how it once looked and pictures of the family in the old days. And Mervyn has taken the photo of his mother—Joyce. I don't think he'd ever seen it properly before in our dark room at *Featherbys*, but in this bright light and since you cleaned it, it looks wonderful. He kept staring at it, so I gave it to him. It was taken a year or two before she was married, and she looks so pretty in it, not at all how Mervyn would remember her, if he remembers her at all."

"Did she change a lot?"

"Oh yes, what with unhappiness and illness...she did," Violet sighed. "She and Mervyn lived at *Featherbys* while Gerald was at the war, you know, and when he came back he took them away to a wretched run-down flat in one of the inner suburbs. There was such a housing shortage after the war...it made things very hard. Poor Joyce must have hated that flat after all the space here, and Mervyn, too...there was no garden to play in. Gerald drifted from one job to another and couldn't settle down.

In a way it wasn't surprising that Joyce became ill."

"I suppose Mr. Bottomley would have mixed-up feelings about *Featherbys*," said Sophie, "even if he can't remember much. I bet he was happy playing there when he was little, like Vicky is now. But then, being taken away like that when he was five and not allowed to go back and then his mother getting sick—it might have all seemed like a punishment, mightn't it?"

Violet stared at her. "You could be right, Sophie. I suppose he must have confused feelings about the place, because it was a very sad time, too, and there was anger as well. Poor Mervyn."

Mum's eyebrows shot up when I told her about the latest developments. Bott was set fast in our minds as a greedy, scheming land-grabber and it was hard to try and think of him in any other way. It was as though his character had been set in cement. At least I hadn't been the only one with a bad opinion of him...everyone else had been the same to start with. Mrs. Jackett had said that Gerald Bottomley had poisoned Mervyn's mind against the Featherbys, but the poison had gone further than Mervyn—it had soaked into all of us a bit. And maybe the source of the poison had been the snobby old Featherbys themselves who'd decided that Gerald Bottomley wasn't good enough for their daughter. To them, Arthur had been the big hero dying in the desert, and Gerald and Mervyn could never come near him. But for all we knew, Gerald could have been a hero, too, zooming around in a bomber or something—but that was never mentioned. Maybe he'd had some bad times that made him hard to live with later. I've seen war films with planes being shot down and airmen being burnt to death in their cockpits. Things like that would be hard to forget—they'd give you nightmares.

"Well," said Mum, "it shows how easy it is to misjudge people, especially when you don't know the whole story. Mind you, I still think Mervyn Bottomley is a pretty unattractive fellow and he doesn't make it easy for anyone to like him—but who knows, now that some of the barriers are coming down, he might improve. I guess that like most people he just wants to belong somewhere."

"It's lucky for him that Violet is the one who is left and not Alice," I muttered. "If anyone can improve him and help him to belong, it's Violet."

Chapter 32

uess what!" Ben shouted when I staggered in from school a few days later. I stared at him. I hate guessing games. "It's to do with the Pyles," he prompted.

"They're having a baby...quads, maybe," I tried, thinking of the most unlikely thing. The Pyles didn't have time to have even one baby.

"Wrong! Well, I don't think they are...but anyway that's not it. Look through the window!"

"Not another asset," I groaned.

"Yeah," crowed Ben, "but not the hot-air balloon, worse luck!"

There, at the end of the Pyles' drive was a wine-red deluxe camper.

"It's the sort that has solar power and a microwave and a shower!" grinned Ben. "I went and had a peek while they're out."

"They're off the planet!" I shrieked. "When will they have time to go camping? And where on earth are they going to park it?" Then my brain clicked. "Oh boy, I bet they've been counting on buying the block from Featherbys for their asset-park, especially since the fire, and now it's not for sale! And I bet Bott is too embarrassed to tell them!"

"Well, they'll soon know," said Ben. "The news is all over the front page of the local paper. It's just come."

He was right—there was the headline, NEW PUBLIC GARDEN FOR BOTTLEBRUSH, with a photo of the ruins of *Featherbys* after the fire. I grabbed it and read the report right through. Dad was mentioned several times as "Councillor Huggins, spokesperson for the Bottlebrush Council." He was also mentioned as one of "the alert neighbors who saved the elderly Featherby sisters from their blazing house" on the night of the fire. The fire had been reported in the paper the day after it happened, of course, but the whole thing was described all over again here. It said that the Fire Brigade Chief had since commended the neighbors, including several children, for their actions at the scene.

"The rats!" I snarled at Ben. "They might at least have mentioned our names!"

Then there were a couple of paragraphs about the Featherbys, "one of the earliest families to settle in the district" and "how gratifying it was that Miss Violet Featherby was now making it possible for the Council to acquire this historic site with its magnificent old trees for the benefit of the people of Bottlebrush." There was no mention now of *Featherbys* being a Disgrace or an Eyesore or of its giant trees spoiling the skyline.

Two weeks later a sign went up on the Pyles' front fence:

FOR AUCTION—THIS IMMACULATE PROPERTY REPRESENTS A RARE OPPORTUNITY FOR THE DISCERNING BUYER TO ACQUIRE A FIRST-RATE ASSET IN THIS DESIRABLE LOCALITY.

We made vomit noises every time we walked past it.

Chapter 33

*A*t school, Mr. Scrooby was usually surrounded by swooning kids, but one lunchtime I went back to the classroom to grab my jacket and I found him alone there getting something ready for the next lesson. So I was able to tell him he was right—there really are ideas for stories all around you, if you keep looking.

"Absolutely, Jess," he agreed as he stuck some Creative Writing charts on the board with pushpins.

Then I told him about my holiday—how we rescued two old ladies when the house next door burned down, and how one of them died from a heart attack and we went to her creepy funeral, and how we uncovered an antique Italian fountain and made it work again, and how we helped to save this old garden from being sold to developers, and how we'd had to keep Bott and the Pyles under surveillance, and how we'd discovered things about the history of Bottlebrush and the Featherby family—that one of them had eloped, and another had been killed in North Africa, and another had probably had a tragic love affair...I'd got that far when Mr. Scrooby swept up his papers and gave me a funny look as he hurried out.

"Ah, yes—keep it up, Jess," he said, as though I'd been toiling away on a homework assignment. I could tell that he didn't believe a word I'd said—he thought I'd made it all up!

That's when I decided to write down the whole story of the Featherbys, to describe how it happened while I could still remember everything. But probably I'll never show it to old Scrooby. I'm not so keen on him anymore.

Chapter 34

The Christmas holidays came and Violet moved into her unit. The Council hadn't begun work on clearing the old garden yet, so sometimes we crawled through the hole in the fence and sometimes Uncle Leo and Mr. Jackett would stop by, too, to check on the waterlilies and to top up the fountain.

The gray empty space where the house had been was fast greening over. Among the weeds a few strange seedlings came up, waving two and then four and then six tiny leaves on tough little stalks. We showed them to Mr. Jackett.

"Well, will yer look at that!" he chuckled. "After all this time!"

"What d'you mean? What are they?"

"Let's see—there are five or six gum trees and quite a few wattle trees in that lot. My glory, there's nothing like a good fire, yer know!"

Sophie and I stared at the tiny plants and then at each other. Deep down underneath *Featherbys*, our own old country had been patiently waiting to return.

Publisher's Note:
About Cricket

*B*en and Robbo play a sport called "cricket" through-out much of *Featherbys*. Terms like "demon bowling action" and "cricket stumps" refer to this ball and bat game. Cricket is not widely played in the United States, but is very popular in Great Britain and Australia.

This is how cricket works:

Two eleven-player teams compete against each other on an oval, level field. Two "wickets" are placed 66 feet apart near the center of the field. Wickets are made up of three sticks (or "stumps") that are pushed into the ground vertically so that they stick up 28 inches. Two wooden sticks called "bails" balance on top of the three stumps. Two players from the same team stand in front of the wickets; these players are called "batsmen." The batsman at the outer wicket has a paddle-shaped bat. A member of the opposing team called a "bowler" (similar to American baseball's pitcher) stands between the two wickets, then pitches the ball towards the batsman at the outer wicket; the bowler's goal is to knock the bails off the wicket and make it difficult for the batsman to hit the ball. The batsman tries to hit the ball to protect the wicket and to score runs.

If the batsman hits the ball so that it bounces or rolls across the boundary of the playing field, he scores four runs. If the ball sails over the boundary without touching the ground, the batsman scores six runs. If a batsman hits the ball far enough so that he and his teammate at the other wicket can exchange places, the team scores one run. A batsman is "retired" (like baseball's "out") if the ball is caught in the air by the other team or if the bails he is protecting are knocked down. A good batsman can score many runs before he is retired. Games are often limited to six hours of play, but sometimes can take days to complete.

About the Author

Mary Steele is one of Australia's most successful and best-loved writers for children. In addition to FEATHERBYS, she is also the author of ARKWRIGHT (winner of Australia's Children's Book Council Book of the Year for 1986), MALLROOTS PUB AT MISERY PONDS, CITIZEN ARKWRIGHT, and A BIT OF A HITCH. Steele has lived in Australia all of her life, and has worked as a children's book reviewer, librarian, and freelance writer. She lives in Melbourne.